Shadows in the Mist

A Short Story Anthology

by
George Turner Smith

Copyright © 2018 George Turner Smith

ISBN-13: 978-1725649361

All rights reserved. No part of this publication may be reproduced, stored in a retrieval system, or transmitted in any form or by any means, electronic, mechanical, photocopying, recording or otherwise, without the prior permission in writing of the publisher, except in the case of brief quotations embodied in a book review.

To

my grandchildren

Tildy, Phoebe, Jesse, Ashley and Kieran

Contents

Author's Notes vii

Advance to Mayfair. 1

Sercle and Flash. 10

A Study in Deception 19

Anna Perez. 23

Ribbons. 32

My First Day at School 44

Seacoal 49

Sketches. 59

Breakwater 65

The Sparrow and the Hill 70

The Tapping on the Line. 88

Jaguar and Panther 96

Your Friendly Neighbourhood Club Man
(*With an appreciative nod to Chaucer's 'Friars Tale'*) . . 100

Saturday Matinee. 109

The Wreck of the Hesperus 119

Tour Bus 132

Bombardment 133

Author's Notes

I have always been a frustrated writer. Life and, particularly, the need to make a living for my family has taken me in a different direction to where I had planned to go as a teenager. It wasn't until the family grew up and I had some spare time on my hands that I was finally able to indulge myself. By then I was under no illusions as to the extent of my talent. Being so long out of the game I had to learn all the most basic writing techniques almost from scratch, and so went back to school to acquire the skills I needed to give me a start. Some initial success with my short stories fooled me into thinking this was my best bet at seeing something I'd written in print. I quickly learned how difficult it is to find a market for fiction regardless of how good it might be, and I'm not claiming mine was any good. My trouble is that I need an audience. I am not the sort of writer who writes for his own amusement. I wanted my material to be read (and hopefully liked) by others. While in the process of writing fiction, I also started producing factual pieces for magazines and these seemed to curry more favour with publishers. In particular, there seemed a hungry market for anything to do with railways. This, inevitably, indicated which direction to take, since railways are one of the loves of my life. Six published books and numerous articles down the line I have no complaints. However, sitting around in my filing cabinet were all the stories written over a period of twenty years which had never seen the light of day – or at best a limited light, and I wondered what to do with them.

Hence this book, which as you will have gathered is a personal conceit.

About a third of the stories are based on memories from my Hartlepool childhood, a third from my thirty years living in Selsey in West Sussex and the rest bric-a-brac. I leave you to work out which is which.

I would like to acknowledge the people who helped in the production of this book: my friend Roger Moore (no not that one), his brother Chris who set the book out for publishing and my own brother Jeff who did the fine drawing of the Gormley beach people which adorns the cover. I would also like to thank my wife, Maggie, who assisted whenever I got into trouble with both computers and word processing – which was often.

Advance to Mayfair

It is my birthday and I collect ten pounds from each player.

Another pink slag sunrise lights up the room, casting crimson shadows on the sterile stony world beyond the faded curtains. I stood by the window waiting for the crash while the ovens are being pushed. No-one, apart from me, takes any notice. It is only as darkness engulfs the landscape I turn away and joined the others.

The board, held together loosely with Sellotape, is laid out in the middle of the table, leaving just enough space for banknotes. Regent Street, Whitechapel, Fentonville Rd., the names meant little to me, nor to anyone else in the room other than, perhaps, Dad who was stationed in London during the war. It doesn't matter. It is the handling of all that meaningless money that is the attraction.

Dad is a dog and I'm a ship. Rita's the boot as usual. Mam, a car, lands on Community Chest and takes a trip to Marylebone Station. She doesn't pass 'go' and doesn't collect £200. Mam never did have any luck as far as money was concerned. This was the template for her life and she had her own routine for getting by. Dad would hand over her his wages on a Friday. This lasted until Tuesday when she got her family allowance. Wednesdays we ate leftovers, whether it be Corn Flakes or baked beans. Thursdays Mam borrowed from Aunt Annie to tide her over until pay day. That was how it was, week upon week without exception. I heard that, when my Nan died, Mam was left a bit of money. If that is correct then the money was all gone by the time of our Monopoly nights. The continuing problem for the north-east working man. Dad's wage was too much to entitle him to income support but too little to live on. So, Mam did whatever she needed to do to get by. This continual 'getting by' went some way to explaining her reluctance to part with money even if the cash she handled was just pretense. The rest of us waited patiently, knowing exactly what Mam was about to do. She sat there, biting her lip, agonizing over having to part with 'Bank of Neverpay' notes. Where did Dad's wages go? After all there was only the three of us. In contrast to Rita, motherhood eluded Mam until middle age when, like a reprimand for procreative indolence, I duly appeared.

She didn't buy Marylebone Station. Stations were another luxury she couldn't afford.

Our hostess Rita, by contrast, loved spending. She spent whatever she got her chubby hands on as fast as she got her chubby hands on it. 'Withhold nothing', was Rita's motto. If you've got it then flaunt it. Trouble is, Rita never had it. That was her problem. Always one step ahead of the creditors. She played Monopoly the way she lived, stumbling along from financial crisis to financial crisis, snatching anything that came her way, regardless of worth, like some blind shopper in a January sale. Her home was a living tribute to trivia. She boasted the world's biggest collection of tat. On her sideboard, chipped porcelain figures in ballgowns danced the days away, while stucco fisherman angled for stucco fish in cracked stucco ponds. The mantle-piece specialty was plastic egg-timers; a wide selection of these, the centerpiece a vase of plastic flowers marked 'A special gift from Seaton Carew'. Above the fireplace, terracotta geese were flying past a Victorian copper bed pan, each goose impaled to the bare plaster by two-inch masonry nails.

Rita bought Leicester Square. Small and dumpy, Rita was nonetheless larger than life. She filled space the way liquids do.

Her husband Gerald (the top hat), by contrast, was smaller than life. Only truly visible in good light, his reedy voice was expelled like phlegm from his reedy body. A skeleton with a voice that sounded like a badly tuned wireless. His face displayed more lines than a marshalling yard and he made the worst of what little he had by not putting his teeth in. In consequence, his head had the appearance of a deflated football. In my child's imagination Rita and Gerald were the husband and wife in those naughty Donald McGill postcards I'd sneak a look at, at our local paper shop. Loud, lumpy Rita and weedy-weeny-weaky Gerald. Still, unlike McGill's mean-spirited matriarch, Rita was a laugh, and had a fund of off-colour jokes and stories which she trotted out without embarrassment in front of us children. I remember she always had a great line in double entendres. I never knew anyone else who could generate so many crude meanings out of the most innocent words or phrases. She especially relished the names on the Monopoly board, her all-time favorite being 'Water Works', along the lines:-

"I see you've landed on my 'Water Works'."

"Your big red engine is in my Water Works again".

Or, with a furtive glance across to Mam, "You'll have to watch your old feller. He's got his eyes on my Community Chest."

At such moments Mam would turn the colour of fresh slag but would try and smile, unlike Rita's husband whose narrow angry eyes flitted rapidly between 'dog' and 'boot'.

Dad, of course, laughed until he choked and I tried not to giggle, pretending I hadn't got the joke.

Rita never won at Monopoly. Her acquisitive personality dictated the way she played. The properties she purchased, like the contents of her home, were a mismatched collection of worthless junk. She was always one throw of the dice away from destitution.

We take a break while Rita, goes off to make sandwiches. Her kitchen is tiny, one of only three rooms in the prefab, on an estate of prefabs dominated by the nearby steel works. Stirred from my seat by an angry glance from Dad I offer to help. From the far side of the kitchen door there is a growling response from Rita's two Alsatians. The snarls turned to yelps as Rita kicks them aside to let me in. Her kitchen, unlike the living room, is not 'kept special' for visitors and I gag on a rolling wall of smell; a potpourri of dog shit, old fat and dirty crockery. As I make to retreat, muttering excuses about hearing Mam calling, Rita grabs me by the arm.

"You're a lovely boy our Tommy. Your Mam's really lucky having a lovely boy like you." She hugs me close to her doughy body, placing a wet and unexpected kiss on the top of my head. "You go help your Dad. I can manage.". I assume, being male, I am a novelty to Rita. Despite having more children than Dr. Barnardo's, she only ever produced girls. As she releases me I get the distinct feeling there are tears in her eyes.

Dad and the others have gathered round the piano.

Most of the notes on the keyboard didn't work but it didn't matter much because Dad couldn't play anyway. No, to give him his due, Dad could play – after a fashion. Very much his own fashion though. He never learnt to read music and therefore embellished his inability with overblown flowery accompaniments. The song he was crucifying today was "MY, MY, MY, DELILAH…"

Pauline, Rita's eldest daughter sings along. A pasty-faced girl, a year younger than me, she is standing one side of the piano cradling Rita's latest baby in her arms. Her head is bent forward so that her lank stringy hair falls over her face. Pauline always reminded me of the kids you see in the NSPCC posters, a sad assortment of bones and neglect. She sings enthusiastic but awful backing to Dad's enthusiastic but awful playing, her thin voice submerged beneath Dad's fat baritone. Pauline's position in Rita's household is house drudge. She is the real mother to all those children. If there is an errand to run or a nappy to change it was Pauline who does it. Even so I have never once heard her complain. She is the living representation of Tom the cabin boy in the Captain Pugwash stories I read. Someone who runs the whole show but smiles and said nothing whenever plaudits are being handed out to others. She makes the best she can of the poor hand life has dealt her.

Her cards today include Trafalgar Square and Piccadilly Circus. She wins second prize in a beauty contest and collects twenty pounds; an excuse for Rita to pull apart the front of her cardigan baring, like huge pink aubergines, the frightening enormity of her breasts.

"I ought to be given that, our Pauline," she said, "cos my tits are bigger than yours". This time everyone laughs, including I am surprised to note, Pauline, whose squeaky giggles end in a fit of coughing. She is always coughing. All the kids in the prefabs cough. It goes with the territory, like the black beetles under the sink.

The Council hid the prefab estate from the rest of the town. This was the last refuge of bad tenants. A slagheap shanty town, there are no decent roads here; just dirt tracks that weave their slimy way through a scarred landscape of scrap metal, weeds and spoil heaps. My family had long since moved away to the new estate on the edge of the town, but the prefabs are still my spiritual home. When I was small I played here with the other malnourished kids, building castles and forts out of heaps of waste and litter. Mam would stare at me through the curtains then, waiting for some excuse to drag me indoors, away from the other children with their sallow skin and emaciated bodies. Usually she would claim to have seen a rat, although I never saw one myself. I doubt there were any rats on the prefab estate. Even rats must have standards.

Dad lands on Community Chest and Rita, predictably, chips in with, "You've got this thing about chests you have", and the walls vibrate beneath one of her belly laughs. Dad pays a ten pound fine rather than take a chance and Rita says, "You can take a chance with me pet any time". Dad loves the bawdy banter, but Mam isn't so keen this time round. I can tell that because she forks out £300 for Bond Street, which is of no use to her but ruins one of Dad's sets.

Gerald throws a six and collects a 'Get out of Jail free' card, and Dad makes some comment about Gerald better hang on to the card after the game has finished because he might need it later on.

Like most of the locals, Gerald had had his run-ins with the boys in blue. The prefabs had a deserved reputation for the pettiest of petty thievery. In God's ledger of larceny, the bad lads of the estate wouldn't merit a note in the margin, but they had one defining and perhaps surprising quality, they confined their criminal activities to their own patch. For some reason I could never understand they only burgled the homes of friends and neighbours. This meant that the same sad booty was recycled between households. It never seemed to occur to them that nobody there had anything worth stealing. Mam once told me that someone once broke into one of the prefabs and, finding nothing worth nicking, ripped the gas cooker off the wall and took that. Later on, when the occupants returned and switched on the lights they blew the house up. This was the extent of prefab villainy.

Gerald ignores Dad's sound advice and trades his 'Get out of jail free card' for fifty pounds. I agree with Dad. The card would have been handy to Gerald if it had been real. He was about as good at thievery as he was at finding work. He'd once been caught stealing part of the chicken-mesh security fence around the steel works. He'd bundled his ill-gotten gain up and was loading it on to an old pram when the security 'watchies' caught him. He got six months for that. Other 'bad lads' might cut through a security fence with intent to commit a robbery. Only Gerald would get nicked trying to steal the fence.

I am thinking about this as he hands in his 'Get out of jail free' card to the bank, and suddenly have this image of him being apprehended in his failed fence felony. The steel work's 'watchie' I picture in the uniform of the Monopoly board policeman, whistle in mouth, shouting 'Go to jail – go directly to jail – do not pass go – do not collect £200' and, before I can prevent myself, I start giggling. Gerald looks across at me and I can tell he knows what I am thinking. There's this look of hurt in his eyes, as if he might have expected better of me.

Gerald, who never paid tax in his life, gets an income tax refund of £10.

The fire is getting low and Dad offers to get coal from the bunker out the back. Rita goes off to make another pot of tea and the game momentarily pauses. Mam is playing on the floor with Rita's kids. She loves little children and seems to momentarily come alive, crawling around on the dirty lino, playing with dolls at the instigation of the toddlers. I am watching this when I feel a hand on my arm. It is Pauline. She pulls me towards the small back bedroom which she shares with her sisters. "What's up?" I ask. She puts a finger to her lips and waits while I close the bedroom door before reaching under the bed and pulling out a small wooden box. She beckons me over. The box must, at some time, have been used for jewelry, as it is made of polished hardwood with a fine carved lid, but the lid is now damaged and hangs at an angle from a single hinge. I assume it had also once produced music because, when she lifts the lid a jerky arthritic, but now silent, ballerina appears and pirouettes before us.

"It used to play a tune, but now it's broken," she tells me. She holds the box protectively against her breast. "It was Mam's. She gorrit years ago. It's mine now though."

She looks warily towards the door then rummages in the box, lifting a thin layer of cardboard that lines the base.

"This is me," she produces a cracked black and white photograph of a small child holding a teddy bear. 'And this is our Karen. This is our Sylvie. This is our Lizzie.' There follows a seemingly endless collection of faded family prints.

"And this is our Chris," she finally produces a photograph of a young smartly dressed Gerald standing beside a thinner version of Rita with a baby in her arms.

"He died," she adds matter-of-factly.

"Tommy", Mam calls from the other room.

Pauline put the pictures away and slips the box under the bed. The others have returned to the Monopoly game again.

"What you two been up to?" Rita enquires lasciviously, "You're not old enough yet for that sort of thing." She smacks her lips loudly, reveling in our embarrassment.

The game restarts and I go back to Old Kent Road.

Nobody but Dad is doing well, and Gerald is losing badly. His few possessions are heavily mortgaged and there are few safe places left to land on the board. Dad, as usual, has acquired all the best sets and it is only a question of time before he wins. Gerald shakes the dice angrily and lands on 'Chance'. He snatches the card, hoping for a financial lifeline and reads out loud, "Advance to Mayfair". This is one of Dad's sets, bristling with hotels. The fine, for landing on Mayfair, is more than enough to wipe Gerald out, but for some reason, Dad takes pity on him, taking away only some of Gerald's remaining cards, leaving him some inconsequential utilities. He even gives Gerald a few hundred pounds from the huge pile of notes in front of him,

"Just to keep you in the game," he says smiling.

Gerald stares at the money for what seems like an age then to my astonishment starts to cry. Enormous tears roll down his cheeks and he wipes them over his face with a grubby arm before turning to me,

"Money'll get yer owt won't it? You ask yer Mam and Dad. They'll tell yer. If yer've the money yer can buy owt." He rolls the fake money Dad has given him between his fingers.

"From sale of stock you get £50," he says.

Sercle and Flash

Deer Si

Got here OK. Beach is nice but lots of stones. We are in tents. I share with two Brummies. You'd laff if you herd the way they tork. They seem OK tho. We all went in the sea. Some of the others can swim. Food good. Get our uniforms tomorrow. Love to yor Mam and Dad.

Mike

25th July 1937
Leader

Another batch of cadets arrived today. As you might suspect they're the usual mixture of pasty faced, malnourished, detritus. Our priority was to get some decent food inside them since they are of no use to us in their present shape. As suggested, after reveille, we held games in the Windmill paddock. I did my best to match like against like, using a team made up mostly from the kids from Stepney against the rest. The cockney kids are good at cricket but too skinny to take part in the more physical stuff. However, I spotted one or two useful looking lads in the boxing.

I hate to raise the subject, but we are going through Central Office funds at an alarming rate. It is obviously out of the question to complete our programme of events using only the subs. collected at the camp. The outfits still have to be paid for. Not surprisingly, from the kids' point of view, the candy floss stall does better than the bookshop. We organised a march through the camp today and many of the local village residents came out to cheer us. Inevitably there were the usual couple of lame-brained malcontents but by and large the locals seem supportive. I would like, therefore, to arrange a formal rally in the village. Please let me know if you can find time in your busy schedule to favour us with a visit. You may be assured of the warmest of welcomes. Who knows we might even be able to find you a decent bed !

regards

B.D.

Si

You won't beleeve what time we get up in the morning. There's a horn that wakes you up and before you can get brekfast you have to do P.E. I was shivering like mad till we got going. Got to say tho the food was grate. Bacon and eggs and as much tea as you want. After brekfast we kitted up and they sorted us into platoons, just like the army. I'm a cadet leader because I did allrite at boxing yesterday. They had us marching up and down on the beach and gave us banners to carry. It was really boring. But after they took us down the shows in the villij and I went on the dojems. 2d a go !!!!!!!! There was a barny with a few snotty kids from the villij who were corling us names. No problem for my platoon you mite gess. A few sore heads in the viilij last nite. After tea they lit a big fire on the beach and we sat round singing songs. Some toff from London made a speech about forenners nicking all our jobs. I can't remeber exackly how it went but it seemd to make sense at the time. Someone passed round ciggies so it could have been werse.

Mike

27th July 1937
Leader
Hope you are well. The weather has been kind and the camp activities have consequently benefited. There seems to be a spring in the step of the recruits to the youth and cadet corps, not apparent when they stepped off the bus the other day. It is amazing the effect of a little wholesome food, sanitary living conditions and a disciplined lifestyle can work on kids destined, without our help, to a life of drudge and indolence and possibly crime. This camp is merely a taste of the kind of improving and invigorating holiday that is going to be the birth-right of every man woman and child in the realm once we are in power.

The improvised latrines, unfortunately, need some work.

Bill's introductory speech was well received. He's a fine orator and would have a great future on the BBC if he wasn't committed to the movement!

You've probably read the text already (assuming you didn't write it in the first place) but he explained how organised Jewry conspired against the interests of the British people and how uncontrolled immigration is stealing the bread from the mouths of the poorest in the land. He was the first person I'd seen wearing the new uniform and I must confess to being impressed. The shirt and breeches were spotless and his boots gleamed. Afterwards some of the officers made up a small party that went down to the fairground in the village. You can imagine that in front of the 'local yokels' we cut quite a dash. I won a coconut and Bill a goldfish, which he magnanimously handed over to a youngster who followed him around throughout the evening.

You may be amused to hear that some of the boys are producing a satirical paper, provisionally called 'Bilge' for the benefit of the camp. It all looks fairly harmless, with one particularly sharp article drawing unfavourable comparisons between the present Westminster lot and the gap-toothed Slavic peasantry. Obviously, I'll keep a fatherly eye on it to ensure that it contains nothing too controversial.

Looking forward to seeing you on the 1st.

B.D.

Camp Commandant
Si
The rally in the villij was grate. There was more than 200 of us marching up and down the rode like soljers. There was a speech by some posh bloke with a tash and we all lined up behind a band dressed like jocks with bagpipes. Bluddy orful row. There was qite a turn out to woch us. We went down the high street past the shops and on to the beech. Everyone waved and cheered. I was at the front of my skwod carrying a flag. There was a bit of a punchup at the end cos a gang of red nutters started throwing stones. Our bodygards waded in and gave them a good hiding. Blud snot and teeth everywhere. What a laff. I even helped out !!! Youv no idea what a grate weppon a flag is if you aim for the face.

When we got to seafront we all sang the nashernel anthem and then had to hang round for ages while old tashy got changed sos he could go for a swim in the sea Youd kill yorself – the tide was rite out and he had to work out miles before he even got his bluddy feet wet. There was a competishen using pebbles to see who cud make the best sercle and flash. Thats our baj. We won and tashy shook my hand and sed I was a credit to the moovment. The wethers grate. Red hot. Wish you were here.

Mike

30th July 1937
Leader
I can't tell you what a pleasure it was having you down here on Saturday, a huge morale booster for everyone. The speech you made raised can only have lightened the spirits of all lucky enough to hear it. I genuinely believe the days of the present government are numbered.

What wonders we can achieve once we're in power! My mouth waters at the prospect. I spotted two or three journalists from the 'nationals' amongst those covering the event and they couldn't fail to have been impressed. You stand head and shoulders above the other party leaders in terms of charisma. The Mail is already on-board. I pinholed their man who confessed to being a big supporter of the movement, since he fought in, and had bitter memories, of the last lot. I pointed out we are the only major party still committed to peace. I think we should make this our main argument over the coming months. We must be seen by the World as a non-violent movement, with room for all regardless of race or background.

By the way there was some trouble after yesterday's parade. Nothing the stewards couldn't handle of course but the sort of thing the press could make a meal of. One or two minor casualties amongst the local hotheads.

Classes begin in earnest tomorrow and I am enlisting Bill to assist. I know you think his views are a little extreme, but he is your most dedicated follower and a stirring speaker. I have divided the boys up so there is a mixture of new recruits and senior badge carriers in each group. I don't want the subject matter to get too intense; we are not dealing with Oxford graduates here. A little simple economic theory with examples they can relate to should suffice.

I will keep you informed of progress.

B.D.

Si

Boring day. Boiling hot and stuck in tents lissening to some fat toff spowting off about Hitler and Musserleeny. You shud have heard him going on. Waving his arms about and going red in the face. Never thort about it much before but I did see his point. Everyones eqwal in Jermany not like here. The Jermans don't need the vote cos theyve got a strong leeder to show the way. If we were the same wed all get our fair share of the reddys out of the pockets of the jews – no offens – Ha Ha – just repeeting what he said. Ive been singled out as a leeder. I wuddent mind a yuniform like the speeker had. All lether and silver. After class I took my sqwod up the villij for a drink or 3. Went in this ruff bar what was just like you see in cowboy films. All went qwiet when they spotted our shirts. No trubbel this time tho. The bastards are to scered to take us on exept if they can cach us on our own.

Mike

2nd August 1937

Bill

Thanks for coming down at short notice. M. is a decent enough cove in his way, and has power and influence in all the right circles, but his views as to the direction the movement should take are too wishy-washy for my palate. I know you feel the same and are harbouring thoughts of leaving the party. Please reconsider. We need all the good people we can muster. God knows we have enough enemies – not least the hook nosed Jew-boys of the press who regurgitate the lies that keep our main potential allies, the proletariat, at a distance .

I gather you are off to Berlin next week with Unity. If you have the chance, and knowing Unity I suspect you might, try and gain an audience with the man himself and explain what we're trying to do here. A little financial support would not go amiss. Remind him, should he need reminding, that the guttersnipes we wine and dine at the camps are drawn from the same source material he used himself when he started.

Talking of the 'gs', I think we've unearthed a diamond amongst the coal – a kid from the east end, built like a heavy-weight boxer, popular with the boys and immensely malleable. The only drawback, having seen his letters home, is that he appears to be mates with a second-generation Semite. This is a problem we will need to overcome.

Looking forward to hearing the latest on our friend across the sea when you get back.

B.D.

3rd August 1937
Leader
You will shortly be receiving a detailed breakdown of the income and expenditure for this year's camp and will note that the Eldorado Ice Cream franchise was a notable success, as was the sweet and gift shop. The bookshop was less successful, and I feel it might be worth trying something different if we are to get the message across to the lower orders. Have you considered, for example, some simple device like getting peppermint 'rock' made up with a 'circle and flash' through the middle.

I think that boy from the Clapham branch, Michael – you may remember me mentioning him to you – looks just the sort we're after, handsome, athletic, handy in the ring, moderately intelligent (after a fashion) and dedicated to the cause. I have already appointed him to his own command, a small platoon of like-minded 'East Enders'. I can see him eventually wearing the insignia of the elite guard . I have had a few words with him, however, about the company he keeps outside the movement and I think he got the picture.

We have just one more week before we all go our separate ways, but I can confirm this to be our most successful camp yet, due in no small measure to your own support and personal appearance. However, we must capitalise on what we have achieved and I would suggest that the local conveners waste no time, on returning home, in getting the boys out on rallies and marches in their assigned patches. Events overseas suggest we may be even closer to government than at any time since the party was formed; but we should proceed with caution until matters resolve themselves. As I have said before, at this moment in time we must be seen to be the only peace movement. However, if, during the course of an otherwise peaceful parade, the odd shop window gets broken, well that's just the way of things. We can attribute such trivialities to over-xuberance or, better still, the infiltration of communist agitators.

Hope you and your family are well

B.D.

Simon

Got your letter this morning. You forgot to include that cutting you menshun cos I cudn't find it. The papers make all that stuff up anyway cos theyr scered of us. It dusnt matter who you are here as long as your on our side. Its your lot tho thats pushing us into another fukking war. When we get back to London the sparks are gonner fly. I cant tell you how cos its suppost to be a secret. Your family needent werry we arnt going near your place but some other jewboys are gunna pay. Sorry I cant come to your birthday party next week cos theres a branch meeting that nite. To tell the truth I dont think Ill have chanse to come round at all for a wile what with all the rallys and stuff but you can cownt on Ill be in tuch.

    Michael

From 1935 to 1939 annual summer camps were held along the south coast by Mosley's 'Union of Fascists'. Touted as free holidays for children of deprived families they were, in actuality, recruitment centres for the Blackshirt movement.

A Study in Deception

"I think we all need to believe in something don't you? I still think Elsie and I just provided a public service. Nonetheless I find it amazing how gullible some people are. I've never told anyone the full story before though you will be aware of at least some of the details. It was the summer of 1917. My cousin Elsie and I were playing in the loft when we found this old box camera amongst a load of photographic equipment; developer, fixer, the lot. Dad must have dumped it all there years before. We bought a film for the camera and took it out into the garden to play around with it. It was one of those lovely hot summer's day you don't seem to get any more. There wasn't a cloud in the sky and the hedgerows seemed to be humming with life. That first picture, the one that caused all the fuss, was only meant for Mum and Dad. They got so excited when we showed it to them and made us explain in detail where we'd taken it. Anyway, Dad must have sent the picture to the paper because the next thing you know there's a reporter at the door wanting to talk to both of us. They took our photos and the following week we were front page news in the local paper. After that it all got a bit silly. Overnight we became famous and to tell the truth we loved it. Celebrity gets to you- you know. If you've never experienced it, it gets to you. Even later, when people were getting more sceptical it was good. Notoriety is still better than not being noticed. Anyway, we felt obliged to give the public what it needed and we went on and made a second and a third and so on."

The old lady closed her eyes and drifted away again. For a while the only sound in the room was the wind stirring the heavy drape curtains at the open window and the clack, whirl and chime of the grandfather clock by the door. She stirred and ran a leathery hand through her thinning silvery hair.

"There was nothing very clever about the way we did it you know. In fact ,we found it all too easy. Elsie cut out the shapes and I painted the figures. I was rather proud of them to be honest. We just copied illustrations from children's books. If all those reporters had been good at their jobs they would have identified the figures we used in the books on the shelf in my room near where you're sitting now. We took the little figures down to the edge of the stream and fastened them to bushes or stuck them in the ground. We always made sure there was either Elsie or me in the pictures for scale. Nothing too clever really. If you look closely you can even see the sticks on which the cardboard figures were attached. You wouldn't think it would fool anyone. Especially Arthur. Not someone who had written all those clever detective stories. What was it his man used to say? 'If you eliminate the impossible then anything that's left must be the truth'. Something like that anyway. But I think, like all the rest of them, he wanted to believe. His wife had recently died, poor man, and he needed assurance there was more out there than what the eye could see. His great friend Houdini was the same I understand. Oh Arthur? Well he turned up one day out of the blue. By then, we'd made the nationals and I think he'd read some article about us in the Times. He was really interested in the paranormal then.

Used to conduct séances in his house, that sort of thing. Mum and Dad were star-struck of course. He was very famous then, still is I suppose, and he made us explain every last detail about our great 'discovery'. Of course, we just made it all up. We told him the little people came to see us every summer but this was the first time they had allowed us to take their pictures. Complete rubbish obviously. We said that it was no use anyone else trying to photograph them as they wouldn't appear to anyone else. Only us. There was a steady stream of people after that, pilgrims I suppose, who just wanted to sit near the brook and be near them even if they weren't privileged to see them. You would be amazed at the number of people who did see something though – even Arthur.

Something that was part of our childhood became part of our adulthood and the poor pilgrims never stopped coming to the cottage. Elsie and I never meant it to go on as long as it did but once you tell a story it acquires a life of its own. In the end to tell the truth would have hurt too many people we loved, particularly Mum and Dad and poor dear old Arthur. So, we kept up the lie and the lie eventually became the truth. I think even Elsie believed it all towards the end. Over the years we were asked about that summer of 1917 lots of times and were even invited to give talks with slides to learned societies. We were even interviewed by the BBC, did you know that, but we never told the complete truth. Never went back on the promise we made that first time. In the end I wish we'd just stuck to that first picture – you remember – the one by the waterfall, but the world kept wanting more. You can't turn the clock back can you? We gave them what they wanted. That's how it was. I'm happy though to finally get it all off my chest so I'm glad you came. Perfect timing. Mum and Dad died years ago, Elsie died last year – did you know? And now there's no-one left to protect."

When the man left Francis's eyes filled up. Through the tears she watched the tiny figure rise from its favourite place, beside those notorious pictures on the bookshelf. It didn't look back as it flew to the open window and out into the garden where it all began.

Anna Perez

1 May

my nameAnna
  hate this place
  hate old lady
  she teach me Inglish words.
  she make me rite down what hapen says Nattely not forget.
  I live with her now.
  before I live in happy hot place with other kids.
  then we live in big house.
  lots of boys lots of girls in big house.
  solyers say you stay in big house now.
  say mother and father bad men.
  say not live with mother and father no more so cry lots.
  all children cry lots.
  then old lady come. bring me here. cold here. I not see frends no more.
  She make me rite inglish words in diry.
  I not rite more now.
  16 november
  Now I go scool. They say old lady my mother. She not my mother.
  Old lady say Nattely you go scool like good girl. I say I am Anna.
  She say Nattely you now my little girl. This cold place. It rain a lot. It rain at home too but not cold. I hate it here.

Old lady say Nattely wash your fase. Nattely come your hair.

Nattely your room a mess. I hate it here. Food bad. Make me feel sik.

December 25

Old lady say today is Cristmas day. On this day all good children get present. This day Jesus get born she say so we get present. I get doll. white doll, with yellow hair that speaks werds when you pull string. I call the doll Anna. I have doll in other place with kerly hair called Saffy. Soljer. say give me that old rag and take Saffy away.

I like Cristmas in this cold plase. Better here now. Old lady show me picher of boy and gerl. She say Nattely you see these children they were my children they died but God has given me you now.

I sit on old ladys nees and she holds me tite and crys.

At nite I think of home and mother and father but not cry so much now.

June 21

Today it was hot. Not like home but OK. I am in class 9. Miss Edwards is nice. She tells us stories. I draw a lot. Miss Edwards says 'Natallie what are these men doing'. I tell her they take children away and put homes. They take mothers and fathers away. They shout and wave guns. I tell Miss Edwards about old home. Father was kind man. We had peeple who cleaned house drove me to school in big black car. My mother say father is pleeceman who catch bad men. not like pleeceman here. He tell other pleecemen what to do. Soljers come to house. Father say 'Anna you go and play now'. Old house was nice better than here. It was hot.

There was a swiming pool. I had dog called Pabby but not see Pabby after soljers come. I miss Pabby.

January I

Today is the first day of new year. Janet and I visit her sister and brother who live near sea. It is so cold my hands tingel.

Huge waves, big as houses, land on promenard and leave weed on road and pavement. Janets sister says I must call her Auntie Meg. She gives me a peace of cake and a glass of wine. The cake tastes heavy and is covered in yellow stuff called marzypan. I can understand most of what people say. They talk about me. They go into the kitchen but I hear them thro door. Auntie Meg says 'Whatever made you do it Janet. How were you going to manage' Janet says 'I couldnt leave her in that awful place. Most of those kids end up out the streets'. I only hear a few more words. Auntie Meg ask Janet something and she says '5000 pounds'. Later we go to Janets brothers. His house also near sea but smaller and dirtier than Megs. There is washing on line which goes across road at back of house. I think Uncle Bert doesnt like me. His wife speaks to Janet but not to me. There is a baby in pram and two other children. The boy is called Paul. He is nine like me. He says Youre that blackie that Aunt Jan brought back arent you. Where did you live before. I tell him. I say I also live near the sea but there the beaches clean and the water blue not grey like here. Paul say if I dont like it why dont I bugger off home then. Janet says I think its time to go Natallie go get your coat. I stick my tung out at him as we go and he makes V with fingers. He is rude boy.

September 9

I am back at school again after a long holiday. Janet has not been well and I help with the cooking also looking after the house. I find it hard now to remember my real mothers face. I have no picture of her. I still get homesick sometimes. One day I was crying so much Janet took me to the libry and got some books for me to read about my country. I do not know the places or people in the book tho sometimes I see a name I seem to know. Janet said she found me at a home in a place called Santiago and said that my parents are dead. I don't believe her. I was werried about the first day back at school but each day is better than the last. I now have two close freinds Sophie and Claire. Sophie has fair hair and blue eyes with very pale skin, Claire is dark like me. I am good at games. I am in the hockey team and run races for the school. I get called names less these days and am near the top of the class in most subjects tho my English is still poor.

I see Paul sometimes.

He is taller than me with red hair and very white skin. One day he showed me a picture of Janet beside a pram on the path beside his house. Janet looked much younger and fatter. I asked him about what had happened to her children and her husband. Paul said he never heard of any husband but he was told that her children had died.

January 1

Paul was at the party round at Aunt Meg's. We played a silly game called sherards. When it came to my turn I had to mime a book called 'A Tale of Two Cities'. Paul kept getting it wrong. His first go he said "Uncle Tom's Cabin" and everyone laughed except Janet. Next attempt he said "Sanders of the River" and we all laughed again. Janet didn't laugh at all in fact she went red in the face. When he said "Noddy and the Naughty Gollywog" for his last go Janet told him to shut up. Just like that. Everyone looked at her. I felt awful.

October 6

I was walking back from school today when I ran into Paul by the gates of the boy's grammar. I said 'Hi' and he looked around carefully to see if anyone was watching before replying.

"Look", he said "You live with my Auntie Janet so that's fine by me but that don't mean we're friends. I never asked for a nig-nog for a cousin so you leave me alone and I won't bother you OK?" I never said anything to him, just walked away. I wasn't going to show him how hurt I was. When I got home Mum could see I had been crying but I never said what was the matter. I sat on my bed later staring into the mirror on the dresser. Why did God make my skin black?

June 20th

I ran for the County today in the Northern Counties Challenge. I got the silver in the 800 metres and won the 1500 metres. Mum was in the stand cheering. When I took the silver up to show her there in the stand was Uncle Bert with Paul. Uncle Bert said,

"Well done our Nattely."

Our Nattely ! I couldn't believe it.

Even Paul smiled but I made a point of ignoring him.

When I came out of the changing room Paul was waiting for me. I tried to walk past him but he barred the way.

"I want to tell you", he said "I couldn't give a monkeys what colour you are. That day I called you a … called you names I was only upset because you are a girl and I knew me mates were watching."

He then stood to one side and as I brushed past him he added,

"I hope we can be friends Natt".

I walked away without looking back.

May 6th

I have just found this diary amongst some schoolbooks Mum had sorted out from the loft for the tip. The last entry must be from my third year at the secondary school as there is a reference to the hockey team which I joined in year 2. Sophie Richardson moved away to Birmingham two years ago and we've lost touch, Claire Timpson I still see, although less often.

I know a lot more about my former life now than I knew then. My fathers name, apparently, was Perez and he worked for the government in Santiago. Mum doesn't know what happened to him but she thinks that my family became separated as Pinochet purged the country of radicals and potential opponents. Mum has promised that, when it is safe to do so, and when we can afford it we will go back there and try and trace my family.

December 20th

Mum has to go into hospital within the next few weeks for tests so I will have to stay with Uncle Bert. I love the situation of their house on the seafront. It looks out straight on to the long curved breakwater that always reminds me of a long concrete arm wrapped protectively around the little flotilla of fishing boats in the harbour. I still get mesmerised by the great waves that sweep in with a 'crump' to break over the pier in an angry arc. The ocean trying to reclaim the land. In winter the air is heavy with sea fret and the shingle is heaped across the edge of the neat municipal gardens on the Headland. Paul and I used to dare each other to run to the end of the breakwater and back; timing our runs to avoid a soaking from the foam flecked rollers as they broke against the concrete wall. We would wait for the crunch of the wave striking the rocks below us and then cling to the railing as a great wall of water rose slowly over our heads before crashing down, hopefully, in front or behind us. We were forced to abandon this game after the newspapers reported two boys being swept away and drowned but I can still feel the thrill and terror as I wait for the thump of the sea on the sea wall.

July 31st

I recall my old home now only in dreams. I have this recurrent nightmare in which I am hiding behind a woman (my mother?) skirt as the uniformed men kick their way into my room. Someone is screaming and I am pulled out of her protective arms. I am aware of the rough feel of an army jacket on my cheek as I am carried away. How much is real and how much is fantasy, constructed from the terrifying images in Mum's history books, I have no idea.

June 17th

I am staying at Pauls' place.

Paul is away at University. It is a strange feeling. Someone's bedroom is an intimate place and I feel uneasy and embarrassed. The walls are covered with posters, mostly concert promos for new wave and punk bands I don't recognise. They jostle for space beside 'arty' Athena posters showing young couples., hand in hand, wandering blissfully through dappled sunlit landscapes.

June 21st

I opened his wardrobe yesterday and found pictures of naked girls pinned to the inside of the door> White girls with big white breasts. To my annoyance my feelings are those of jealousy rather than shock. I stand in front of the wardrobe mirror and compare my body to the girls in the pictures. A skinny dark girl looks back at me – flat chested and childish. I pull my stomach in and strike a pose like the girls in the pictures. I look ridiculous.

January 21st

It seems appropriate to add a final brief note to this journal. I don't suppose I shall ever find out now who my real parents were. Paul and I were married in August and at my instigation we spent the last few months out in Chile being shunted from one bored Ministry official to another. The man I thought was my father had had some prominent position in Pinochet's secret police. I had been acquired by the childless Perez family when my true parents were 'disappeared'. Following the restoration of some sort of democracy the state made a half-hearted attempt to identify stolen children and restore them to their families. These were the soldiers I remembered. I seem to have ended up in a children's home, the 'San Marcos' in Santiago as I found the following brief reference amongst a list of over a hundred names,

'Anna Perez – girl brown hair brown eyes – aged 5 to 6 years'. There is no reference to any formal adoption.

May 27th
Janet died today.

June 12th
Paul and I were clearing out Janet's things when Paul came across some papers in a holdall in the loft. Amongst dozens of small prints of dark skinned children there was a picture of a small sad faced little girl. It was stapled to bill of sale which read:-

'Anna – 6.5000000 pesos PAID'

Ribbons

Luther wondered what the harbour looked like without the sea. The tide was creeping back in across the marsh. Invisible at first, it rose silently through a swirl of marram and sea purslane, emerging suddenly in a shimmering ribbon stretching from the harbour mouth to the flour mill.

He opened the sluice gate to let the sea in to the mill pond for the last time.

The dark marsh slid quietly beneath the waves and the wading birds moved away until silence returned to the wetland. The marsh slept once more, waiting for the moon to pull the ocean back over the shingle bank so that the dense whirling flocks of birds could return and feed.

Luther sat down with his legs dangling over the harbour wall gazing out across the water, its surface still flecked with the drowning stubble of marine plants, as waves pulsed into the tidal pond with increasing vigour.

He could clearly hear the auctioneer's voice,

"18 pairs of grade 1 stones. I'll start the bidding at 5 guineas. Do I hear 6 guineas. Seven guineas. Ten guineas..."

During the years Luther's father ran the mill the stones were in constant use; grinding out 40 tonnes of flour each day. Luther wondered how his father would have felt, knowing that from now on the tidal movement of the sea was not to be harnessed.

The sea nosed under the rusting water wheels. These were to be sold along with the rest of the fixtures and fittings.

The mill would never reopen. The sea, the life force of the mill, was about to be barred from the harbour forever and the land reclaimed for farming.

***

Luther's earliest memory was of being carried on the shoulders of Tom Arnold, the chief miller, up the steep wooden steps to the upper floor where two young apprentices were loading grain into the feed silos. The boys, stripped to the waist, were barely visible in the swirling cloud of hot tan coloured dust. Their daily task was to drag the sacks from the pulley that ran from the ground floor to the top of the mill, clamber on to a narrow platform above the hopper and pour the grain down the throat of the mill engine. Luther could hear the boys now calling and waving to him through the dappled haze, their bodies streaked like the pelts of wild animals, ribbons of sweat running down the flour paste on their skin.

The working day always began with the ebb tide.

The mill workers gathered in small groups, waiting for the signal that the tide had turned. An extended metallic groan was the signal that the mill wheels were beginning to move, and for the next six hours the mill rocked with activity. Water from the sea-charged pond was fed through narrow wooden channels running alongside the building to spill over the mill wheels, and thence back into the creek. Latterly, a small steam engine was also used to keep the mill active during the intertidal hours but on that day, many years ago, when Luther first visited the mill, the works moved only to the diurnal breath of the sea.

At 'high water' the men loaded flour on to sailing barges, whose shallow draught, permitted working the narrow, dredged, creek from the harbour wall. Those long dead mariners from Luther's childhood were now calling to him,

"Don't just sit there young-un grab one on them sacks."

'You keep the tally Luther there's a good lad.'

"Sundry wagons and carts – as seen – do I hear 3 guineas, 4…"

The bargees voices faded.

A garland of pintail duck whirled around the harbour calling to each other, their eerie call – like spirits from phantom sailing ships calling out when the sails of the boats were unfurled to meet open water. The duck settled, en masse, below the shingle bank that shielded the harbour from the sea. The bank had naturally extended year on year but would soon be artificially seal off, isolating the harbour forever. The pintail were usually the first to arrive. There would be goldeneye later and the tiny green teal. Mallard and shelduck were always last but would stay rooting in the mud long after the sea had departed, harrying returning wading birds competing for feeding rights on tiny islands of mud and marram.

The church bell rang the hour.

***

"One o'clock Annie," Luther said to himself, "Kids'll be home soon."

Luther met his wife at the church.

The Sunday visit to St. Mary the Virgin was essential to social life in the village. It was a rare opportunity for young people, from far-flung hamlets, to meet. The agricultural labourers and their families were crowded together in plain wooden pews allocated to their employer, who sat starched to attention in his own ornate padded box directly in front of the pulpit.

Luther moved amongst them – heard their creaky tuneless hymns beneath the pastor's deep baritone – sat down with the jumble of short stocky men bursting out of ill fitting once-a-week suits. Women in plain brown frocks and red and blue woollen shawls – and those startling hand made bonnets garlanded with garish ribbons.

And there was Annie.

She was standing at the end of the pew; slightly apart from the rest of her family, in the section reserved for the farm workers, her face half hidden by a prim white bonnet tied with a silver ribbon that bobbed in time to the congregational responses. During the service there was a commotion as a pigeon, trapped in the rafters, made a feather-shedding attempt to escape. As it fluttered frantically in the roof above her she turned her head and for an eternal second looked directly into Luther's eyes.

Framed by the silver ribbon was the most perfect face Luther had ever seen.

***

Luther tried to recall how she looked then, barely eighteen – chubby heart-shaped face with the flame coloured cheeks of a farm girl – the complexion of summer and those deep set blue/green eyes like sunlight seen from the ocean floor.

"Silver ribbon", Luther muttered to himself.

***

After the service Luther waited outside the church and approached the girl's father, casting furtive glances towards the smiling girl with the downcast eyes at the back of the group.

"Good morning", was all he could think to say.

"My name's Luther Barnes and I live over at the flour mill". He said he would be pleased to show any of the family round the mill after church one Sunday trying not to stare so obviously at the girl in the white bonnet. Her father looked at the boy and then at his daughter, who was blushing with embarrassment. The following week Luther was permitted to show Annie around the works which were closed each Sabbath. He led her through the creaking dusty building, rambling on about anything that came into his head – the downturn in the value of corn – the relative merits of different types of lifting gears – anything to cover his shyness. The girl said little, occasionally nodding or shaking her head. Up and up the flights of narrow wooden steps between the working platforms they climbed, Sometimes, their bodies would touch as he helped her up through one of the narrow intervening trapdoors.

Luther could feel that tingle in his hands after all these years.

On the uppermost level he held her waist to support her as she climbed up on to the feed silo platform to look from the small window out across the harbour. As she stepped down she slipped, falling into his arms. For a moment longer than really needed he held her in his arms.

"I'm sorry", he said.

She looked up at him. "I'm not", she replied.

"Stay exactly where you are", said Luther and rushed off, vanishing into the depths of the mill. From below she heard mysterious cranking noises, thumps and rattles and suddenly the mill came to life. All around her cogs and wheels were turning. In the centre of the platform a heavy wooden spindle supporting the top millstone began to turn.

"Mr. Barnes", She called out, "Mr. Barnes – Luther. Where are you? Don't leave me here".

Moments later a wide trapdoor set in the floor and linked to a pulley in the roof of the mill opened as if by magic.

"Luther – Luther stop playing games", she shouted into the mouth of the trapdoor. Like a pantomime villain Luther burst out of the hatch. He was riding the pulley, one foot and one hand linked into sack loops fastened to the wide leather strapping. He released his grip as soon as he cleared the trapdoor, landing nimbly on the balls of his feet in front of her.

"At your service", he made an elaborate bow and Annie applauded.

They were married the following spring.

Luther's father gave the young couple the cottage overlooking the harbour. It had been partly derelict for many years and over the next three years Luther repointed the stone walls, replaced the copper coloured roof tiles and in his spare time fathered three children, Luther Junior, Rebecca (Becky) and Matthew. Matthew had been a difficult birth which had left him with learning and speech difficulties. Despite his handicap, he was the only child with a real love for the mill. From infancy he followed his father around as he worked or, more often, would be found sat beside Tom Arnold listening agog to the outrageous stories the old man told. As a toddler he had the annoying habit of getting under the feet of the usually patient millers who would swear and swipe out whenever they tripped over the small tousle haired boy. Gradually however, almost in spite of themselves, they grew to like and even respect him because, unlike the other bored and fidgety apprentices, Matthew would be happy with any of the simple repetitive task they gave him, provided he was given time off to talk to his beloved Tommy.

Luther Junior was different in every way.

Luther had nurtured hopes that the mill would pass into the hands of Matthew's brighter older brother, but he soon learned that his eldest son's hopes and ambitions lay beyond the great sea wall. When Luther came home from work he would find the wiry dark-haired boy at harbourside talking to the bargees or just staring out across the marsh to the open sea. On the days when the boats were not able to get dock because of foul weather the boy became moody and withdrawn.

Luther taught his son the rudiments of writing and arithmetic hoping to hand over the accounts to the brightest of his children, but Luther junior's mind was elsewhere. The only time he showed any interest in the lessons was the day Luther read him the story of Noah from the huge leather-bound family bible. He remembered the boy running his hand over a faded tinted picture of the ark; the masts broken and the rigging in tatters, the boat wallowing in the trough of a giant wave. In the background a stern God looked on.

Becky was the liveliest of the three and also the most difficult of the children to comprehend. At meal times she would be the last to appear; having wandered off somewhere and lost track of the time. Late in the evening, as he worked alone in the mill, he would hear Annie's voice calling out across the harbour for the girl to come in to supper. With the passing years she developed from a lovable but rebellious child into a distant introspective adolescent. One day not long after her fourteenth birthday, she did not respond to Annie's evening call and Luther and the boys spent a cold miserable night combing the fields around the mill for the girl. The next day Annie found a short note in Becky's room, written in her characteristic backward sloping hand. It read,

'Dere Mum an Dad

I am in love and have decided to leeve home so Joe and I can be together. Do not wherry about me. I am happy and safe. I will collect my things when things is sorted.

Love you lots
Becky'

It was six months before they heard from their daughter again. One Sunday, after church, there was a knock on the door and there she was – slightly taller, slightly thinner but mostly pregnant. It seemed that she was living just a few miles away with a married man who had promised to get divorced and marry her provided Luther would give his consent. There was an angry exchange between father and daughter and she walked out of his life for ever.

***

Luthers' eyes misted,
"Never meant it Becky – you know me?"

***

A year after his daughter left home Luther's father died. He had been ill for some time and his last rational act was to sign over the deeds of the mill to his son. Unfortunately, along with the mill, Luther inherited his father's debts which were substantial. The old-fashioned tidal mill was now competing with steam driven industrial equivalents. The modern mills were faster, more efficient and totally independent of the vagaries of wind, sea, or rain. They were also, unlike the tidal mill, built closer to their potential market. As the price of flour fell dramatically, with the running costs of the mill increasing year on year, Luther was forced to lay men off. Within a couple of years, the total workforce consisted only of Luther, the two boys and Tom Arnold.

One day Luther came down to breakfast to find his oldest son dressed in his best suit and packing belongings into a canvas bag. It was hard to fault the boys' logic,

"You knew I'd go to sea eventually Da". I've the offer of a merchanter , 'The Lucknow'. She's laid up in Portsmouth. This is right for me Da. The mill don't produce enough to keep all on us. I'm happy my share goes to Matty. I'm sorry to leave – really Da, Specially now things is so bad, but it's all for the best. I've told Mum. I'll keep in touch and send money back when I can. Sorry Da".

As he turned to leave Luther called him back and for as long as the boy would allow him he hugged his oldest son. Finally Luther Junior pushed his father softly away,.

"Got to go Da."

Luther walked with him up the lane as far as the village where they parted.

Autumn had turned to deep winter when Luther and Annie received the first postcard. It had an Indian stamp and said simply,

'India very smelly. Work very hard but not too bad. Love to Mam and Matty. 'L'.

That was five years ago…

"The final items for sale may be purchased separately or as a whole. They consist of the following : one double and two single beds, good condition: one oak armchair, one ladies mahogany dressing table…"

***

Annie died of consumption. She had had a cough for a few weeks but had made light of it; blaming the September sea mists which she said were 'getting on her chest'. That horrible bubbling cough, got steadily worse, especially at night. When she began to lose weight Luther took her to a doctor in the City. By then it was too late. For a few months he watched her waste away until one bitter frosty night she died suddenly, without dignity, in the middle of a violent bloody coughing fit.

Matthew never did understand where his mother had gone.

The doors of the mill finally closed for good one spring morning, the day the Brent geese left the harbour flying north to their nesting grounds in Siberia. Fortunately, by this time, Tom Arnold had retired. Luther led his youngest son for a last look around the silent buildings. He had arranged for his son to live with his sister in Southampton. There was talk that they might find him labouring work on the docks but Luther thought it unlikely.

"Tide's out Da'. Shall I do the Sluice?"

Luther shook his head. He took Matthew's hand in his own holding on to it tightly,

"How do you fancy living with Auntie Edie, Matty?"

"Auntie Edie could come and stay here and help us with the mill couldn't she Da?"

"She lives a long long way away Matty. She could use a useful lad like you. She wrote to me and said , 'Please could Matty come and live with me and help me out 'cos he's such a good lad.'

"Are you coming as well Da?"

"Sure – course I am – soon as the mill is all sorted out."

The mill was put up for auction the following month.

✶✶✶

The tide was turning. Marsh grass was starting to reappear and the flocks of duck were lifting off the water in impatient hurrying swathes.

"That concludes the business for the day. Thank you gentlemen."

✶✶✶

Navvies were working on the flood bank next to the harbour. Ballast was being laid. down The railway was coming to the harbour but too late to save the mill. The deepwater creek would soon be too silted to use but then again it no longer served a purpose.

Luther got to his feet and walked the few feet to the door of the tidal mill. The auctioneer had gone and the building was deserted. He opened the door and went inside locking the door behind him. The mill looked little different to that day he had shown his future wife around for the first time. The old man sat down on the bench where Tom Arnold used to tell Matthew stories and for a while stared ahead at the specks of flour dust dancing in the angled shafts of evening sunlight. Then he stood and walked across the room and swung over the lever that controlled the sluice. Water rushed through the gate and the wheels began to turn. He looked around the building for the last time. It was good to see everything working properly, a ribbon of old flour fell from the turning mill stones and on to the wooden floor.

My First Day at School

It is my first day at school, so Mum is cutting off all my hair.

As the long blonde tresses fall to the floor I start to cry.

"It's alright love, don't worry. It'll grow back, you have my word".

She dabs my eyes with the edge of her pinafore, "Remember it's only special children who get to go to school. I'm very proud of you".

I hide my face in her breast and sob.

"Come on Tansy, there's a good girl". She lifts my chin, "Give me one of those famous smiles".

There's the clump of heavy boots on the stairs.

"That'll be your Dad. Hurry up, they'll all be waiting. Wear your green coat. No, not that one; the one with the fur lining. Don't pull a face. It's the warmest and it will be bitter out there on the hill."

Dad enters the bedroom. His mantle is hidden under his long heavy greatcoat.

He beams, "How's my baby?"

I shrug.

"First day at school. You should be excited. No-one ever forgets their first day at school. I remember mine like it was yesterday. It'll feel a bit strange but once you get to know the other kids and the teachers you'll have a great time, believe me. Remember Tansy – we're special."

I look down at my left hand and wonder, not for the first time, why should I have been singled out by the Gods to be born with just four fingers. I touch the place where the little finger ought to be. Dad is watching me. He takes my hand in his own four-fingered hand.

"Special", he says.

My friends Glyn and Myree are waiting at the door, along with their own parents. We hold hands and stumble our way along the narrow dark lane, past all the familiar rows of flint cottages and our silent village pond. I have never been out this early in the morning and my teeth are chattering uncontrollably already. There are no lights in any of the cottage windows. All the residents are out there on the hill waiting for us.

Gradually our stony lane becomes a rutted muddy track and we pick our way carefully as the light we had had from the full moon is now obscured by a high hedge. The men light torches with Dad leading the way.

There are other groups climbing up the hill from surrounding villages. I can see lines of lights heading to the same place from multiple directions. All are aiming for the stone circle.

I chat with Myree. Myree is very special. She was born with a strange face, with a hole in her lip which makes her talk funny. Dad told me she is Sulis's child, made in Sulis own image, and because of Myree the village will never again want for water. She has lovely dark curly hair which she pins back behind her ears with a gold clasp, although my friend David says he prefers my blonde hair. Most of the girls in the village have dark hair so I stand out from the rest. Not that it matters much now as Myree's hair, like mine, has been cropped. Still. I wish I had her gold broach. I only have a copper broach. Everyone in the village has copper broaches.

Myree's father is a baker and very fat. We keep stopping so that he can catch us up. Glyn says he sounds just like one of those new steam engines that the priests bring to the village at harvest time. Dad tells him not to be so cheeky or he won't be allowed in school. A cat slinks across my path. I stop. I won't move until she has disappeared under the hedge. Myree knows I hate cats, "You are silly", she laughs. I tell her about that time Mum and I went to the town. We had taken a short cut through the old Christian graveyard and I frightened a black cat with her kittens beneath one of those magic stone crosses. The mother cat hissed at me and later that day we got caught in a terrible thunderstorm on our way home.

"Kittens are sweet", says Myree.

"It's alright for you I reply, "Cats like you"

Myree keeps going on about her cat Arthur, named after the hero of Badon. "Arthur", she says, "wouldn't hurt anyone".

The track steepens. We have to hang on to branches of overhanging trees for support. I can see the light from the fires in the distance. There are other men wearing mantles moving in the firelight. We enter an open space where Dad joins a group of men standing next to an enormous bonfire. It is too dark to be sure, but I think this is the Place of the Holy Oaks, where the Gods are said to live. I can smell something cooking. There is to be a feast after school.

All around me are small groups of shivering, whispering children waiting for school to start. A horn sounds, and all the Mums and Dads start removing their outer coats. All the men are in the white of the brotherhood. All except my Dad and Myree's Dad who wear the royal purple. Miss Bennett comes over to where we are standing. She is one of the elders

My First Day at School

and wears a red sash that only partially covers her dumpy red breasts.

"Right children", she says, "take the hand of the person next to you and follow me. Form a straight line. No Talking Gyn please".

The adults line up either side of us. I take Myree's hand and we walk between the great standing stones to the centre of the Holy Place. Dad is already in position behind the alter stone, trying to look serious and important. He waits until we are inside the circle before speaking,

"Good morning children and welcome to your first day at school. In a moment the first lesson will begin. Some of you are perhaps cold and hungry but remember there are hundreds of children throughout the land who would gladly change places with any one of you. You are the chosen ones -those that the Gods have marked out for their service. Today, as you all know, is the shortest day of the year. It is the most important day of the year for all of us. Without our prayers the Gods might never wake from their winter sleep. The seeds would not grow nor the crops harvest. We, the brotherhood, are the thread that links God to mankind. Without the science of the priests there would be no steam engines, no corn mills, no mastery of metal that gives us both the plough and the sword. Do not betray this gift children. Each of you will one day share in all this knowledge and in turn pass it on to the next generation. This is the glorious cycle of life as willed by the Gods.

"And now we begin".

Behind Dad there is a red glow and the horn sounds again. At a signal from Miss Bennet all the children take off their clothes and we stand shorn and shivering in the centre of that great ring of stones. After what seems like an age a sliver of sunlight appears behind the alter stone and Dad smiles encouragement at me. The ceremonial knife has been placed in the centre of the alter stone.

"Tansy come forward please", he says.

My big moment has arrived and I stand before the alter my head bowed.

He reaches behind him and places a wicker basket on the alter stone next to the knife.

"Gods of earth, sky and water accept this humble gift".

From inside the basket he produces a fully grown and obviously pregnant black cat. Pinning her head to the stone with a gloved hand he exposes her throat. He looks at me,

"For the Gods", he says.

I reach for the jewelled knife with enthusiasm.

Seacoal

She always waits until there's football on the box and it's pissing down outside before she starts. It's Newcastle United tonight as well.

'You needn't sit there, there's no coal and the man doesn't come 'til Wednesday."

"Yer joking aren't yer", I complain, "Ah'm buggered if ah'm going out in that."

I point to the window where rain droplets stream down the glass in parallel lines.

"It's your own fault," she says, "you should have gone straight out when you got home. You'd have been there and back by now."

"Alright for you," I say, "You weren't out at 4 o'clock in the morning cycling to bloody work." She takes a duster and starts polishing the sideboard furiously.

"Anyone would think you were the only one round here who worked, the way you talk."

There's no point arguing when she's like this.

"Joe Boagey's on the same shift as you, so's Ronnie Dougan. I bet they don't keep going on about it all the time to their wives."

"Joe Boagey works in the stores and sits on his arse all day. As for Ronnie Dougan he's got a cushy job in the rolling mill. I'm the only daft bugger round here knee deep in shit on the coke ovens."

"There's no need for language like that – in front of the kids."

Tommy's two and Robert's six months but I haven't time to argue before she plays the trump 'cruelty to children' card. "It'll be your fault if them bairns go down with something. Whooping cough's doing the rounds."

But it's pissing down. For Christ's sake," I beg.

"You won't be too long. You'll be gone and back in an hour, Wear your donkey jacket – that'll keep the worst of it off. And while you're out I'll put the tea on so's it'll be ready for you by the time you get back."

I quickly check the 'Radio Times'. The football doesn't start 'til ten so, in fairness. So I can get down to the beach and back before it starts – assuming the tide's right. I check the Evening Mail . Low tide's at eight.

"Oh alright then. I'll see if Joe wants to come."

I shove on me jacket and go next door. The wind hustles me up the path, pinning me against the glass door of Joe's porch. After a few hard thumps on the door, Ruby answers.

"Bloody hell George. Howay in 'fore you drown. Joe it's George."

Joe's stretched out on the settee, bare feet on one of the arms, watching 'Coronation Street'.

"Alright Smudge?" he says without looking up, "Cup o' tea?"

"No thanks – just had one." He looks so bloody warm and cosy I nearly don't have the heart to ask, "The thing is like – I'm off under the arch for seacoal and I was wondering if you'd fancy coming."

He pulls a face, "What. In that?" He nods to the window.

"It won't be so bad once you're out. Low tide's at eight."

"It'll be pitch black by then. How will we see what we're doing?"

"We'll manage. We've got the lamps on the bikes. That should be enough. It's not like we don't know the way."

There's what people on the telly call a 'pregnant pause' as he listens to the rain battering against the window, then he turns to his misses for support.

"You've just got the tea on the go haven't you pet? She's just got the tea on the go Smudge."

I shrug, "Alright Joe. Not to worry. I just thought we could have given each other a hand, like."

Ruby taps her husband gently across the back of the head,

"Go and get your coat yer miserable bugger. You wouldn't let your mate go out on his own in that? What sort of mucker are you?" She looks across at the fire, "Anyway we could use some coal ourselves for 'banking up'".

I don't suppose you've ever used seacoal. If you did you'd know it's bloody awful stuff compared to 'real' coal but it costs nothing and is good for 'banking' with. It burns so slowly it welds itself into a cake that burns slowly all through night. Next morning you just give it a poke – bingo – there's a fire again.

Joe looks miserably around the room, first at the telly, then at the roaring fire and finally at the rain trying to force it's way in through the framework of his window.

"Well alright then, but I'll put a pound to a penny there's nothing doing."

The thing about seacoal is you can't predict where it's going to turn up. I've seen it lying in layers a foot thick and the width of a road. Lying so deep you couldn't fill your sacks quick enough – and better quality than some of the bought stuff too. Other times I might slog along the beach for miles at the low tide mark and see only black stains on the sand. Or worse still, patches of crappy stuff, so full of stones and seashells it bursts like shrapnel as soon as it gets hot.

That reminds me of a funny story.

The Council once tried to turn the estate smokeless. Without asking anybody they went into everyone's houses replacing all the fireplaces with hearths designed to take that stuff called 'smokeless fuel'. Now here's the daft bit. The new hearths were supplied with fancy glass fronts. Course no-one round here could afford the special coal you were expected to use, so we just carried on using seacoal like before. Within a week all those glass fronts had been blown apart, so the Council had to come out again and put the old fireplaces back. Silly buggers.

We meet by my gate.

Joe has put his working clothes back on and tied a woolly muffler over his face. I'm dressed the same. Here we are, the seacoal twins; same black donkey jackets, blue overalls and wellies. Our identical coal gathering kit consists of an ancient bicycle, with coal sacks tied to the crossbar; a battered enamel bucket hangs from the handlebars, with a spade fastened between handlebars and saddle. There's a howling gale blowing off the sea right into our faces. We set off – pedal a few yards – push the bikes a few yards – wait for a lull in the wind – pedal a bit more. By the time we reach the railway arch leading on to the beach we're knackered and soaking wet. The road's paved through the arch but on the far side it's buried in sand and we struggle, head down, through wind-blown dunes like cheap extras in the film 'Lawrence of Arabia'.

The tide's a long way out and it's getting dark by the time we reach the low tide mark. You might guess there's bugger all coal and Joe's all for turning back but I say 'Let's just have a quick look beyond the 'Point' since we've come this far. In any case', I tell him, we can't get any wetter'. I don't know if you know the town but the Point's that bit of land that sticks right out into the sea. The current slows down as it goes past and if there's any seacoal being carried it drops out in the bay on the other side. You've got to get in and out quick though because there's no way off the beach other than scrambling a twenty-foot sand cliff and that's nigh impossible with a bike.

We're in luck – the sand is hard and wet so the wheels barely sink in. We're round the Point and on to the beach in no time. My plan is to have a quick scout around, grab what we can and then get out before the tide turns and cuts us off. But now it's dark and we're working from the bikes' headlamps. There's no sign of coal, just the usual mixture of leathery seaweed, scallop shells and driftwood. Still, we weave up and down the tide mark criss-crossing each other and are half way round the cove when Joe calls out,

"Ayup Smudge."

He's higher up the beach, near high water, which means the sand's soft and the bike harder to push so I'm sweating and wheezing like a steam hammer by the time I get to him.

By the light of his headlamp I see an enormous black drift. Joe's already ankle deep, filling his bucket, and from the speed he's working this is something special.

If you've never used it there's all kinds of seacoal.

Some of it's just like dust – bloody useless really because it just clogs up the grate. Other stuff's so mixed up with shingle it's like putting live ammo on the fire but Joe's found the best, rounded glossy black lumps the size of plums with hardly any pebbles or shells. I wade in to help and we fill the two sacks in no time, tying them off at the neck. I'm for calling it a day then. I'm cold and wet and 'Match of the Day' is waiting but Joe can't believe his luck and is already re-loading his bucket.

I shine me lamp nervously out to sea. The beam falls, worryingly, on water but I convince myself it's only wet sand.

"Howay Joe," I said, "Get a move on. You know how fast the sea comes in here. If we're not careful we'll get caught."

"Just a couple of sec's Smudge. It took us long enough getting here. There's enough coal here to last us a month. "

"We can come back tomorrow when it's light enough to see what we're doing.".

"It won't be here tomorrow – you know that."

"Neither will we if yer don't get yer finger out."

"You always were a 'worrit' Smudge."

He keeps on shoving coal into the second of his sacks but I've had enough and tell him I can't wait any longer.

"Alright then just give us a hand to load me bike and we'll head on back." he says regretfully' looking at the still untapped billows of coal lit up by the bike's light. As soon as the sacks are draped over the handlebars we start back towards the Point. I can see straightaway that Joe's bike is overloaded. The bottom of his front wheel is sinking deeply into the sand and the harder he pushes the deeper it goes. Eventually the handlebars twist away from him and he pitches forward.

"'What the…?"

His lamp goes out.

"You alright Joe?" I call out.

"Bloody wet though." He sounds scared, " Smudge the tide's turned."

I point my headlamp out to sea. Shallow black wavelets are moving steadily towards us.

"Shit – Can you remember how much the beach slopes just here Joe,?"

"Not much I think."

"Right – if we get a move on we might get around the Point before the water gets too deep."

Joe is fiddling with his light.

"I think the bugger's shorted out."

"Forget it," I say, "Just follow me and for Christ's sake dump one of your sacks or you'll drown the both of us."

He moans a bit but reluctantly begins to untie the string at the neck of one of the bags.

"Just dump the bloody sack Joe – we've no time for that."

I'm really pissed off by now and set off without waiting for him. Moments later, however, I'm pleased to hear him splashing along behind me. The truth is though, now it's dark, I've no idea which is the most direct line to the Point so we keep to the tideline to the end of the cove, then keep below the cliff towards the Point. Our luck is in because the beach hardly shelves here but bit by bit the water is getting deeper until finally we're knee deep and the sea surges in over the tops of me wellies . Those of you who only paddle in the sea on summer holidays in Bournemouth don't know how cold the North Sea is in winter. My teeth start chattering straight off and I'm shaking like a riveter's elbow.

Nonetheless I think we're going to make it when there's a noise behind me and it's Joe, gone over again in the drink. I aim my bike to where I can hear him thrashing around.

"Smudge – Smudge for Christ's sake"

To my astonishment only his head and shoulders are visible above the surface of the water.

"Smudge it's 'quickie' Smudge. Give us a hand."

It was my fault of course. By not going in a straight line back to the Point we'd walked into a patch of quicksand beneath the cliff. I kneel down with the freezing water rolling up under my jacket and push my bike out towards him. He grabs the handlebars and I lean backwards to heave him out of the muck. Suddenly the sand lets go and I pitch backwards. Our sole surviving light goes out.

It takes a minute or two before my eyes adjust to the dark then I make out distinct shapes in the black. There's the Point. It's only fifty yards further on but it hardly matters because, on the rocks under the cliff, I can see great breakers bursting against it in showers of white spray.

"Grab yer bike." I howl.

We turn back, slipping and stumbling over submerged rocks. Suddenly a wave bowls me over again and I stand up immediately, gagging on brine that tastes of old cabbage water. I almost abandon me bike but then I think 'Sod it – I've worked bloody hard for this' so I scrabble about under the freezing water find the bike and push on again towards the shore. Amazingly the coal sack survives, bedraggled, from the crossbar. As soon as we reach the beach we flop down on the sand to get our breath.

"What now Smudge?" says Joe.

"Well we can't stay here that's for sure. God knows how far the tide comes in this time of year. We've got to get off the beach."

"How?"

"I'm buggered if I know. We'll just have to have a scout 'round and see if there's an easy way up the cliff."

We haul the bikes up the slope, as far as possible, and we separate to find a way off the beach. It doesn't look promising;

the slope gets steeper and steeper the nearer you get to the top, ending in a grassy, sea cut, overhang.

"Smudge – over here."

Joe's found a rain gully that has cut a wedge into the cliff. It's steep but climbable.

We retrieve the bikes and get back at the same time as the incoming tide.

Have you ever tried pushing a bike loaded with seacoal up a steep sand bank? I hadn't 'til now and the most positive thing I can say about it is that it stops you noticing the cold.

Joe leads the way, splashing through the water and ramming his front wheel into the 'V' notch at the base of the bank. Head down he attacks the slope. His front wheel vanishes immediately into sand and, despite our best efforts, we are only able to shift the bloody bike a short distance. So off comes the seacoal and the bucket and at last, with much heaving and pushing, we get Joe's bike to the top, only to find the turf overhang too wide to overcome. I have a brainwave – grabbing the spade I hack at the turf overhead. I'm showered in earth, but it only takes a few stabs and I'm through. We push Joe's bike through the hole and on to the cliff top then go back for mine. Just in time. My bike's being chucked about and is part buried in wet sand. I wait a second for the sea to retreat then wade in and try to pull it clear.

Joe is trying to get his seacoal out of the water.

"Give us a hand will yer." I shout. He ignores me and continues to struggle with the sack.

"Leave it Joe. If we don't look sharp the sea'll have me bike."

He still doesn't look up so I grab him by the shoulders and yank him to his feet Would you credit it? He's crying like a baby; tears pouring down his cheeks. Fancy – a grown man crying like that.

"Come on Joe," I put my arms around him, "No need for that kidder. It's only a bit of coal."

He shakes his head, "Sorry Smudge. It's just …after all that.

I feel the same if truth be told but this is no time for whingeing.

"Never mind Joe. We can always come back and get the sacks tomorrow. "

He nods but we both know I'm lying. The sea always cleans up anything left on the beach. We stand there holding on to each other, like little kids, until a wave whips up the gully knocking us over like skittles. Spluttering and choking we grab my bike between us and run at the slope as if we were sprint starters in a cycle race. The bike's slung up and over in one movement and we scramble up through the turf tunnel beside it.

For a long time we sit there shivering on that sharp edged bristly turf as the sea crashes in below us, then I find a packet of sodden 'woodies' in me jacket and offer one to Joe. We suck silently on those unburnable tabs for comfort until I can stand the cold no longer and get to my feet.

"I don't think our lass'll be best pleased when I come home with no coal for the fire."

Joe looks up and nods,

"Aye – bit shitty that. Still, you can borrow a couple of buckets off us Smudge – see you over tonight. Low tide's half seven tomorrow. That'll give us more time than we had tonight."

I hadn't thought of that.

Oh – and Newcastle United lost as well.

Sketches

I forget things these days.

Today is Friday. I think today is Friday.

A girl called Pam visits me on a Friday.

I think today is Friday.

Sometimes she brings children.

The boys are nervous. They stare out of the window towards the city. The little girl sits on the edge of the bed. She laughs and tells me stories. She is fascinated by my immobility. She writes me "Get Well" cards.

Pam makes conversation.

She has arranged for the lawn to be cut every other week. The cleaning lady no longer calls. The milk has been stopped. The family are all well.

She tells me the little girl is my grand-daughter. That she has told me this before. The little girl hands me a drawing she made at school. She says it is me. It is a matchstick figure in a bed. A matchstick nurse stands beside the bed. The figures have no bodies, just heads. The nurse's head has a cap with a red cross. All the heads are smiling.

I need to talk. To tell them things. But jumbles of memories muddle the words, like scenes from some old newsreel, the images disjointed, black and white, unreal.

I talk about the war. I was young then, not much older than the boys in the room. The War was significant. I grew up in the War. I have an old picture book from home in the cupboard by the bed. I ask the girl who claims to be my daughter to fetch it out.

The pictures were taken in Southern France during the summer of 1939 when, backpacking with friends, I crossed the Alps from Switzerland to France. Then, because of those events in Poland, I was forced to abandon my original plans and run for the Channel. The trains we traveled on were full of troops – young boys in uniform not much older than ourselves – I recall them staring at us with frightened.

There are no frightened eyes in the photographs, just grainy images of smiling teenagers.

I remember the faces: I forget the names.

If I close my eyes I can see the faces.

I think today is Friday.

✲✲✲

A black nurse comes in, "How you feeling today?", she asks.

I ask if I can go home now and she changes the subject Would I like a drink or something to eat?

A meal appears and I am propped up to eat it. Is this breakfast?

Time is measured in meals.

Some days doctors appear. Some days they don't.

Doctors are what happens between meals – some days.

✲✲✲

Evie scolds me for lying in bed, "Are you going to get up now or what?"

Sundays we go to the park with the children.

Evie and I are walking beside an artificial lake. The children's dog (what's its name again?) dashes in and out of the water. Irritated ducks scatter. The children kick a ball on the grass where you are not permitted to walk. The dog runs ragged figure eights around them barking and sniping at ball and ankles indiscriminately.

Evie reads while I draw. The wind ruffles the grass like comb through unkempt hair. I do my best to capture the effect but today it eludes me. The grassy mound in the park becomes a castle in the drawing and the river a moat. On the opposite bank marching hordes of suburban houses lay siege. The river slithers through the picture, black and cold. Debris from yesterday's Chiltern storms swirl and eddy and I trap them in pen and ink.

✷✷✷

My meal is taken away untouched. I no longer get hungry. I only eat for their benefit. They worry when I don't eat. Sometimes I can't be bothered.

✷✷✷

I remember Normandy. Armored war wagons, clanking and groaning, metal wheels spewing sand on a bloody beach. The shambles of war – children dye in sandcastles – leaderless groups congeal and disperse. Men yell and weep – seeking direction from someone – anyone; noses touching to make their voices heard over the crump-crump of the guns. I can see the incomprehension in their faces now. The faces of the boys on the train.

Beaches are meant for holidays not funerals.

***

I need to see my sketchbook again and reach for the file with my drawings in the bedside cabinet. There is a gap in the sketch chronology created by the war and its immediate aftermath. A photograph left over from my wedding album is pasted in the middle of a page marked '1946'. Here I am tall, slim and proud in my demob suit. Evie is wearing a white cotton shirt with wide padded shoulders and a hat the size of the Queen Mary.

I turn the pages.

It is now 1955, the river looks the same, but the skyline has changed – blocks of flats, like the backdrop to a thirties Hollywood film peer over the shoulders of the rows of Georgian terraces. Stapled to one of the pages I find a faded print of the children; my daughter is dressed for guides, long plaits trail from under a beret; my son, in white shirt and shorts, mouths long forgotten complaints to the camera. I show the picture to the nurse.

"Your two?" she asks. I nod.

I struggle for their names but it's one of those days when names hide in the shadows at the back of my head and refuse to come out and be recognized.

"The little girl is called Pam – her name is Pam", I say with relief but by now the nurse has gone. In the days before my world was this room I trawled it for the inspiration in my sketches. My life has become the pages of this scrapbook.

Old memories are the new reality.

***

I am sitting in the Piazza Del Marco. The sun throws shadows of marble stallions on to a white basilica. Pigeons and tourists flock around while I draw. They preen and squawk and demand to know if my sketches are for sale. They must occupy a two-dimensional world, lacking the feel of the sun or the movement of the sea in and around the buildings.

Gondolas slide under the Bridge of Sighs. Gondoliers sing snatches of well-rehearsed arias for the benefit of Japanese lovers. Their voices fade and are replaced by the ceaseless clatter of camera shutters. The songs disappear into the distance, like the drawn-out exit of a cathedral choir.

I recognize that arch.

There was a stone courtyard just beyond it where a café spilled out on to the pavement. I remember sitting there one long soft afternoon sipping syrup-thick espresso coffee.

The narrow streets shine in the sun. The houses are bronzed and weathered. The colours in the sketch have faded but the colours in my mind are vivid, butter yellow stone arches, pink cream and ice blue stucco houses; like so much Wedgewood porcelain. Oily green canals are there and flickering fiery red fuscias woven into iron railings; cascades of plum purples and succulent tangerines. Colours I could never reproduce in my English garden. I remember taking a cutting from one sprawling rowdy shrub, cultivated it and used it to brighten the corner of my lawn that mostly caught the sun. The plant thrived but the flowers it produced were pale immitations of their Mediterranean parent.

Another sketch.

A castle, like a skewed granite crown, standing defiant on a hill in Provence. A cobbled road winds up the hill from a golden village like the dusty coils of a sleeping snake. I can feel the prickly heat on my neck and taste the velvet soursweetness of the local wine. Barefoot children are watching me from the shadows. I see their tousled dark hair and hear their laughter from the margins of the red tiled houses.

There are some half-hearted scribbles amongst the later pages and I come across the pitted bleak landscape of Skye. It is 1970. Evie had died suddenly the previous year and the children have grown up and moved away. Their absence is there in the landscape. In the foreground a blue road flows over the moor towards the sea, vanishing in a jumble of grey moss-covered boulders. Dark clouds hang over the mountain and malevolent giants watch me from the crags. On the cliff face a stripe of grey denotes a switchback path that cuts across the scree. It twists and turns through granite slabs to emerge in the moss hung amphitheatre of the Quirang. In the drawings there is no escape from the sky. The land cowers beneath it and the rivers run swiftly away.

There are no sketches in the book of Evie or the children. I did not deliberately leave them out. For me they will always be there, standing alongside me, looking into my pictures. The image of my family is clearer to me than the mauve curtains around the bed. I have never felt the need to capture their likeness in pastel crayon.

Evie scolds me for lying there, "Are you going to get up or what? The children want to go to the park." I think it is time to go.

Outside it is getting dark. The streets are long canals of moving lights; yellows pour towards me and reds stream away, fading into the amorphous glow of the city.

I am a red light.

Breakwater

The men were too busy making ready for the fishing to pay much attention to Mary. To them she was another part of the breakwater, like the forlorn brackets for the missing lifebelts.

As the anglers baited the hooks and joked amongst themselves, the breeze freshened whereupon they tied their mufflers a little tighter about their necks. Mary shivered and fastened the top two buttons of her plain brown coat, tucking the collar under her headsquare. It was getting late. She knew she would soon have to leave or risk being marooned on the pier, along with the fishermen, as the returning tide rolled over the section of pier nearest the shore. It was close to high tide now. The tumble of black rocks that formed the beach had long gone beneath the sea. On the rusty red handrail one solitary seagull tilted its blue-grey head back and screamed abuse to the swirling shoals of fish moving into the harbour.

It was cold. It was always cold.

In summer the wind swept in off the North Sea, lining up waves in soldierly ranks, ready for battle with the pocked concrete ramparts of the pier. In winter, as now, this maritime army armed itself with an additional wind-powered battering ram, which it used to assault he seaward side of the breakwater spewing up into the sky in fifty-foot waterspouts, before tumbling over into the harbour in a Niagara of salty foam. Mary would be on the promenade at such times, hands clutched tightly to the rails, heart beating wildly, waiting, for the first bang as the sea battered itself against the stone. The tension would build within her, as the force and bulk of the waves increased, until it seemed that neither Mary nor the breakwater could withstand the onslaught. Then, in a maelstrom of foam, the sea would retreat and there would be a period of calm before the attack began again.

Mary read the graffiti on the walls of the concrete shelter – "Beryl Kirby has big tits – "Tony loves Pat –TRUE", beneath a crude representation of a naked female. She bit her lip and turned to watch the men as they baited their lines and launched them with a whip-like flourish beyond the railings. Outgoing lines whistled the accompaniment to the staccato click-clack of the spinning reels, with the tune ending as the sinkers dropped beneath the surface of the sea. In the summer Mary had watched mouth open, as the men, now stripped to the waist, competed for length of cast. Their bare shoulders would glint and steam under the cold northern sun – athletes in Mary's personal Olympiad. Sadly for Mary, today their bodies were hidden beneath heavy-duty woollen donkey jackets.

Mary dropped the book she was pretending to read into her shopping bag and rose from the metal seat in the stone alcove sheltered from the wind where she often sat. One of the men looked up,

"Bit fresh?"

"Yes." She recognised him. She knew he lived, with his mother, in a small terraced house a couple of streets back from the sea front. He was a few years older than her and she was aware he had once been married, but for some reason the marriage hadn't worked out,

"I don't mind really… though I wouldn't like to stand in this wind all day like you men do."

The man took her in with one glance, her zip fastened fabric ankle boots peering out from beneath her drab old-fashioned overcoat. The face seemed familiar.

"You one of the Searle sisters?"

She nodded.

"I was at school with your Tom."

As he made to turn away she continued, "Tom doesn't live round here no more. Not seen him since he got married. He lives in the collieries"

She moved closer to him. The angler had the ruddy complexion and gnarled calloused hands of the local steelworker.

"Caught owt?", she asked, though she well knew that the contents of his bag consisted of two nice sea bass and a couple of mackerel. She had counted both of them in.

"Not much. Coupla bass coupla mackys – but those stripy buggers give theresel's up without a fight."

Mary was also fishing, "I bet your misses is fed up with fish dinners, what with all the time you spend down here."

He smiled slightly, "How come you know when I'm down here?"

"Ah've seen yer loads of times. Ah just live over there." She pointed towards a row of weather-beaten Victorian town houses on the promenade. She had lived there all of her life. Her parents had died there, and after, one by one, the rest of her family had moved away. The last to leave was her brother Tom, after which her home became a house, dedicated to silent cleanliness. Mary, the youngest, shared the house with a couple of cats and bookshelves of fading photographs. There was nothing to do anymore, no-one to cook or tidy up after, so cleaning the house became an end in itself. There was not one piece of faded carpet left un-swept in the high ceilinged rooms, no section of the oak panelling unpolished. It was as clean as only empty houses can be clean and as tidy as only somebody with nothing else to do can make it.

The man was weighing her up. After a moment's hesitation he spoke, "You can have the mackerel if you want. You can't give mackys away at this time of the year anyhow."

"No I couldn't possibly. 'Sides what'd your lass think?"

"Go on – take them if you can use them. My lot can't stand fish anyway."

He offered her the bag containing the fish.

"Thanks. They're never as nice when you buy them from a fish shop". She leaned closer than necessary in order to touch hands as she took the fish from him. Strong male hands, the middle and forefingers yellow with nicotine, knotted and calloused like the bark of a tree,

"Well I suppose I better be thinking about getting on home." She said without making any obvious attempt to move.

The man couldn't resist a smile. The smile of the successful angler. Admittedly he had had more impressive catches in his time. In this instance he had discarded a mackerel to catch a sprat. He reached into his rucksack,

"Here I've got some newspaper -you know – to wrap 'em in – save messing up your bag."

She hesitated, "Ah suspect yer blue with cold stood here all day. When you finish why don't you come by our house for a cup of tea. Ah've got some photos of our Tom's family you might be interested…"

"Hey up." She was cut off mid-sentence by a sudden tug on the man's rod followed by a whine as the line ran out. The man turned away from her,

"Jack, Bert", he shouted. His friends looked up.

"Big bastard by the look on it."

"Easy Ted – Let her run."

"No macky this time. Codling more like." The men either side offered advice as Ted twisted the rod side to side, first letting the line out then reeling it in rapidly when the tension eased. The butt end of the rod was held between his legs, its top bobbing and dancing in time to the fish's desperate escape attempts. When he judged the moment right he leaned back and a sparkle of thrashing silver broke the surface.

Seconds later the bulbous eyes of a ten-pound codling were looking into the bulbous eyes of a red faced man surrounded by cheering mates. Behind the group of anglers the codling, with its last view of the world, could see a sad faced middle aged woman wrapping up fish in newspaper.

Mary watched the men for a moment or two then walked to the railings and stared out to sea. She opened her bag. The heads of the two mackerel protruded from the end of the newspaper, their dead eyes seemingly scrutinising her. She unwrapped the newspaper and separated the fish which she laid out on the ground in front of her. She folded the paper tightly around them like a blanket leaving only their eyes exposed.

"There now," she said", nice and warm".

Beyond the breakwater another wave squadron leader was assembling troops for one more assault.

The Sparrow and the Hill

The door slammed behind me and I was left alone with the mad woman.

She sat bathed in moonlight on a pile of straw in the far corner of the cage. She looked up briefly but did not otherwise acknowledge my presence.

I would say she was young, late teens perhaps and she wore, I saw, a maiden broach in the centre of her tunic to show she had not yet mated.

I asked if I might sit down and took the chair by the bed.

"Do you know why I am here?" I asked.

No reply – I tried again.

"They say you hear voices."

No reply.

"They say you hear voices", I repeated, "Tell me about the voices."

"Who sent you?" She asked, sounding tired.

"I'm a doctor. I am here to determine your mental state"

She picked up some embroidery from a basket at her side and started sewing. There was a long pause before she replied.

"And you're not concerned if I might be a witch?".

"Certainly not"

She laughed.

"You must think I'm stupid. Who sent you – not the Council by any chance?"

"I told you, I'm a doctor. I'm only concerned with your welfare".

She leaned into the light and I saw her clearly for the first time. I was expecting the usual plain features of a farm girl and was surprised to find a thin faced teenager with a narrow hawk-like nose. She had curly brown hair spilling into her lap the locks of which, from time to time, she fingered nervously.

"Can you describe in your own words what happened".

Silence. I tried again,

"I can only help if you are willing to talk to me. The Council may otherwise condemn you out of hand".

"So it *were* the Council who sent you?"

"Does it matter?"

"Not really."

"Then try helping yourself by helping me."

Another silence.

"If you are not prepared to talk to me then there is no point in continuing – GUARDS"

I stood up.

"I thought it were the River Spirit", she said quietly.

"I'm sorry – what did you think was the River Spirit – the voices in your head?"

She turned around pushing her hair out of her eyes revealing a wide mouth and nervous dark brown eyes that flitted randomly around the cage. When she spoke she exposed white but uneven teeth,

"There were only the one voice at first."

"And you thought it was the River God – why was that?"

She laid down her embroidery, folding her arms.

"Because I were in the temple by the river when I heard it."

She looked into my eyes, and whilst I could see she was frightened, I detected no obvious signs of madness such as facial tics or frequent changes of expression.

I sat down again, waving away the guard who had appeared at the door.

"Do you really think you can help me?" she asked.

"I will try." I replied.

There was another pause, before she began in a rush,

"I were praying in the temple – you know – the old Roman one near where the salmon nets get laid out – over by …"

"I know the temple. You were praying?"

"Yes, it's been a bad year, took barely twenty salmon so far and none of them longer than this," She indicated the distance between hand and elbow," Dad says he can't remember a worse year unless you count the one the year we saw the 'tail-star' or that really dry spring when the river barely flowed. Mum said…"

"You were praying."

"Yes – I wanted the River Spirit to help. It were my idea. Dad wanted us to sacrifice to the Fertility God but She's not helped us much in the past. I don't think She ever comes to our village to tell truth.".

"Just tell me about the voices."

"Like I said – I were praying. It were really hot – sticky – no wind – dead quiet – just river noise – weird – really hot – I were shivering though – scary. I was telling Spirit we could manage on just four middling trout each day and I heard summat – woozy at first – sort of like the wind in the grass – no – more like the sound of pheasant moving through the bracken – nothing really – but weird you know because it were like it were moving towards me. I looked round – couldn't see owt. Were then I heard a voice whisper right in my ear. I nearly wet meself – you can imagine. I've prayed to Gods thousands of times – no-one ever answered before. I thought at first it were Verica, you know – our kid, playing tricks, but this voice were rougher – real nasty. I just froze"

"What did the voice say?"

"See – that's it. I guessed it were a God because I couldn't figure out any on it."

"I've heard the Gods speak in tongues. Only the Council has the wisdom to interpret their guidance."

"I thought that too but it seemed funny a God telling me summat if I couldn't understand what were being said. Then I remembered where I'd heard someone speak like that before."

"Where was that?"

"At street market at Regno."

"Foreign Traders?"

"Yeah – Saxones – their boats come into Harbour every few months. Dad says that there are no finer leather craftsmen in the known world than…"

"This 'God' spoke to you in Saxone?"

"Not really."

"I don't understand."

"What I mean is that it were like Saxone but not like any Saxone I'd heard before. So I thought if this were a message from River Spirit then it must be important and tried to memorise the words even though they didn't make no sense."

"What words?"

"Mostly nonsense but there were two that kept getting said over and over so I thought they must be the most important."

"And those words were?"

"It said 'sparrow' and 'hill'"

"What do they mean?"

"I'd no idea at time but I said I would tell Dad because he would know. Then voice just went away and birds started singing again – weird. I'd not noticed they'd stopped 'til then. I were shaking like mad and took ages before I dared look round again. When I did there were nothing so I flew home fast as I could."

"And you told your father what happened?"

"Course. He believed me about as much as you do. Still, give him due, he came all the way back down to the temple again and we sat there for over an hour listening to the river while it got dark. Then when we gave up and came home. Dad said he thought I were feverish and Mum made a poultice of hawthorn and mistletoe. It really smelled bad and stained my…"

"Did the voice speak to you again?"

"Yeah – not in the temple though. I wouldn't go down there after that. It were nearer to our cottage next time. I were feeding Pinky, our pig. She's a fat thing but really friendly. I only have to walk out into the garden and she runs over. More like one of family really. We've had her for nearly…"

"And you heard the voice again?"

"Look I'm trying to tell you right?"

I confirmed I would not interrupt again

"Like I said, I were feeding Pinky. It were really hot again – air were thick- like oatmeal –like it gets before a thunderstorm. There were muddy clouds hanging over hills and I thought I felt the odd spot so I were in a rush to get inside before the rain came on heavy. Pinky normally gets her head in the slop bucket before I can put it down. This time though she held back, like she does when she sees strangers. I looked over me shoulder – couldn't see nothing.

'What's the matter Pinky?' I said. I could see she were hungry as she kept starting towards bucket, then backing off. I held it out, tipping it towards her so she could see her food. 'Dinnertime Pinky.' I were saying. Then there were a flash of lightning and Pinky turned round and shot off down the hill, heading towards the river with me chasing after her. She went straight into a holly thicket which I thought were real odd. I mean she often roots in the copse but she has a sense about those 'Old God' places and keeps well away from them, same as I do. So I hung around – on the edge of the wood like – calling out to her. I wouldn't have gone further but it started to rain – not normal rain – heavy thundery rain you know. I'd have been soaked through before I got home so I crawled under a bush in the thicket.

It were dark in there but as soon as I got me night eyes I saw I were in a space about the width of our cottage, all surrounded by holly. The branches were all wrapped together, like in a nest – so anyway, I thought, at least I won't get wet. It were just then I realised I were in one of those secret old 'priest' places because there were a stone altar in the middle with some bones laid out in front on it. I didn't look too closely as you might expect. They were too human for my liking – a baby's I guessed. I know it's none o' my business but it's not right is it – killing a baby – I hadn't thought it still went on. Trouble is, Gods seem to longer listen no more so perhaps the Council feel special gifts are needed. I can't have been there more than a minute when I got that same shivery feeling again – you know – like someone was watching me. And then I saw him."

"Saw who?"

"This little boy. He were standing by the altar – skinny kid – about nine or ten I'd say. He were staring straight past me – pale skin, that white Saxone hair and there were black tear-marks all down his cheek. Saddest face I've ever seen – no not just sad – scared too. I felt so sorry for him".

"You have no children of your own do you?"

"No – I've no man. It don't bother me. There's nobody round here I fancy anyway. In any case I get to look after our Briged's two whenever I want to. Little Robin's really sweet she…"

"Did you recognise this child – an escaped slave from one of the villages perhaps?"

"No he were dressed weird – like nobody I'd ever seen before – sort of shiny tunic the colour of sky at sunset and his arms and legs were bare."

"Did you speak to him?"

"Course I did. I said 'You alright?' but it were like he couldn't see me – just went on crying. At least it were like he were crying but I don't remember any noise come to think. It didn't seem odd at the time though. I thought to myself. I bet he's related to – you know – that sad 'gift to the Gods' – so I said, 'Don't cry – your baby's happy now – watching over us – helping us.' He just took no notice. Then I heard those voices. Heathen voices – hundreds – thousands on them – singing to their weird Gods all around – really loud – you know yet perhaps voices were only in my head because I could still hear rain on leaves."

"What did you do?"

"I tried to protect little boy from the spirits so I held out my arms. 'It's alright – don't be frightened' I said and he looked up and I swear he saw me because he suddenly looked like this"

At this point she made a surprised face with staring eyes and open mouth.

"Then strangest thing happened. He put his hands over his head as if to cover himself and sort of crumpled up and vanished."

"Sorry?"

"He vanished – weird – slowly faded away like those morning goblins you see when you first wake up – ones that become furniture when you rub your eyes."

"And then?"

"Then nothing. The voices stopped and I could only hear the sound of rain."

"Did you tell anyone about this?"

"Course. I thought it were another message from Gods so I told Dad like before and of course he went straight to the village priest. – you know – that old fart Ninias. If he weren't a priest he'd have been staked out for wolves years ago. Dad made me speak to him though. and I found him fishing down by river in that old curragh on his. I think he were drunk again because the boat just kept going round and round in circles even though river were hardly flowing. If I hadn't helped him out of boat he'd probably have drowned – might have been best thing as it happens".

"What did you say to him?"

"I told him what I just told you – that Saxone Spirits had been talking to me and I asked him if he knew what those words meant."

"And did he know?"

"He said 'hill' meant mound or mountain but he didn't recognise the other word and he wanted to know where I'd heard it so we went through the business all over again. I tell you he's senile. Do you know he asked me a funny thing? He wanted to know why foreign Gods chose to talk to me. I said he ought to be able to answer that better than me. Anyway he said he would speak to the elders about it.

Well nothing happened for about a week and I'd more or less forgotten about whole thing when I were woken up in the middle of the night by me Dad who said I'd been summoned to 'the Women's Court'. You might expect I were scared stiff. You know yourself, Women's Court only meets to decide what should be done about witches and they never find anyone innocent, or so I'd heard.

They were waiting by the gate. You couldn't tell who were who of course as they all had those carved masks and those long red cloaks that come down over their knees. Nonetheless I soon spotted fat Sybil from Penallt because she can't keep her mouth shut and I'd know her voice anywhere. What does she know about witchcraft? Married to a bloody fishmonger – wouldn't know a troll from a trout. Anyway, I were taken down to the Forum and they sat me in the centre of the pentacle and started firing questions at me. It were freezing cold even though they'd put burning torches all around me. High Priestess did most of talking. She said I were responsible not only for the drought but for the thunderstorm that flattened barley. She said she'd long suspected I were the 'familiar of evil spirits'. I said I didn't know what she were on about and said she would do better trying to figure out what the strange words I'd heard meant than going around accusing innocent people. She told me not to be so bloody cheeky. I could hear Sybil in the background goading her on saying things like 'Listen to her – talking back to the High Priestess.' Eventually I told her straight

'And you can shut up as well," I said, "If anyone's a witch round here it's you Sybilianus'. That shut her up.

Anyway – High Priestess told us both to shut up, then she did this silly dance, pretending to go into a trance. When she 'woke 'she said 'our Goddess of Wisdom' had spoken and that those Saxone 'words' were an infertility curse and I were the 'earthly manifestation' of the curse which is why I can't have any kids. I said she had no idea what she were talking about as Ninias had already told me one of words meant 'hill' so it were a funny sort of curse. Anyway that set them all off. They started chanting 'witch – witch' over and over again. And then whether it were the smell of the incense or the cold or whatever I don't know but I came over all dizzy. The chanting got louder and louder and in the background I heard those strange voices again. I got the terrible feeling there were hundreds of people crowding in on me, crawling all over me, crushing me so's I couldn't breathe. I were being carried along with them. I felt like I were going to be sick and I tried to fend them off. The High Priestess and the court sort of faded away and I were on a steep hill looking down on a flat meadow. All around me were Saxones – smelly, dirty, Saxones – screaming and shouting. The stink of sweat and shit and piss were so strong I wanted to throw up. The crowd moved down the hill dragging me with them until we stopped up against a fence. It were then I saw the little boy again. He were crouched down by the fence with a bunch of other kids all about his age and they all looked really scared like he did when I first saw him.

I tried to get across to them but I were trapped in by all those people. There were this ugly fat man stood next to me. He was dressed the same way as the boy and he stank of mead. 'The kids – look – help the kids,' and I pointed.

The man did nothing – just kept staring straight in front of him with those pudgy bloated fish eyes. Then crowd moved and I couldn't see the little boy no more. All those bodies on me. It felt like my chest were going to cave in and I felt faint. When I came to those silly priestesses were standing over me saying as how I'd condemned meself because I had spoken 'with the tongue of the pagan.'"

"And then?"

"Nothing. Council soldiers came for me next day and here I am."

"Is that all or is there anything more you want to tell me?" I asked.

"Is there anything more I want to say in my defence do you mean? You think I'm a witch don't you?"

"I do not believe you are mad."

"It means same thing don't it. If I'm not mad then I'm a witch. Even worse, a witch who speaks the words of our enemies."

I stood up to go,

"You can be assured I will do my best for you when I report back to the Council."

She nodded and picked up her embroidery.

It was another week before I was summoned to the full meeting of the Council. I had never been inside the Forum before and wasn't sure what to expect. I had heard that the Council moved into the building on the day the last Roman sailed out of Portus. Yet all these years on there is still something awesome about the place even though the marble pillars are no longer white and the tessellated mosaic floor is sunken and cracked. The old High Priest, dressed in purple and wearing a long necklace made of eagle talons, was sat at the far end of the room on a high-backed wooden throne. He has a forbidding appearance; one half of his face was frozen by the Gods leaving him with a permanent snarl. As if this were not enough he dribbles all the time and slurs his words. As a mark of respect for this 'gift' he chooses to shave half of his head so that the left hemisphere of his face resembles the old stone Roman bust that hangs over the Forum entrance. He waved me towards a somewhat less impressive chair placed carefully in the centre of a mosaic depicting some, long forgotten, Roman God with a human body and the head of a hawk.

"Sssit down Bolanus". Half his face smiles encouragingly," Thank you for coming. Gentlemen, Bolanus here issss one of our most eminent practitioners. I have known him for many years and testify both to his extensive medical knowledge and his common sense. How isssss your young family these days Bolanus, especially that young scamp Caius?"

In a less than steady voice I replied that my wife and son were both well.

"There isss no need to look so nervous Bolanus it is not you on trial here. I gather you have reached a decision about the girl."

I nodded trying to avoid staring at the trail of spittle from the edge of his mouth wriggling down his chin.

"And your verdict isss?"

I gazed at the ranks of decayed faces gazing down upon me like buzzards seeking prey.

I took a deep breath.

"It is my belief that Serin is not insane."

One eyebrow raised,

"A simpleton perhapsss?"

"No she seems quite intelligent for a peasant girl."

"Then she isss a witch as we thought".

"I do not think so – at least not in the sense most people would understand the term."

"Explain yourself."

"It is not something I find easy to put into words. If indeed she is a witch then her sorcery is beyond her control. As you are all aware we are in our third successive drought, each drought being succeeded by torrential rain that ruined the crops in the fields. The girl has admitted herself that there are no more fish to be caught in the river and there is precious little game in the forest. It is self-evident therefore that some malign force is at work. It consequently needs little imagination to see that a girl who, by her own admission, consorts with the Gods of our enemies is involved in some way. It is also safe to assume that the thunderstorm that ruined this year's harvest is also connected in some way to her communications with the spirit we can call 'Sparrow'. The inference of action and reaction is unavoidable."

"But?"

"But I still have this nagging doubt that she has any control over events. Rather, it seems to me, she is the unwitting medium of evil spirits."

"And how have you arrived at this conclusion."

"Perhaps her lack of guile. True witches would surely display more cunning."

"I think you give her too little credit for subtlety Bolanus. 'True witches' as you put it would be far too clever to reveal themselves by simple words and deeds".

"Then why did she tell us about all this if she knew it would result in her own death?"

"That issss the only issue that vexes me. Perhaps she felt safe to boassst about her liaisons with these devils to her family. Remember it isss only thanks to the prompt action of her father and the swift response of Ninias that we are able to gather here today."

"Having spoken to her at length I am sure you are wrong."

There was an audible intake of breath from the Council. The right side of the High Priest's face hardened to a mirror of the left.

"Never challenge the wisdom of thisss Council again. You have spent far too long with this woman and appear to have also come under her spell."

"I apologise most humbly if I have caused offence. I just feel that if you spoke to Serin you might reach the same conclusion that I did."

"This Council hasss every intention of speaking to her. What sort of court is it that permits no self-representation of the accused. For your information she isss waiting outside at this moment. Guards – bring the girl in."

It was the first time I had seen soldiers in Roman uniform and, despite my nervousness, I was impressed. The guard was preceded by a ram's horn fanfare and they entered the Forum clad in what must have been authentic armour consisting, as it did, of polished bronze chest plates, pleated leather skirts and feather plumed helmets. The two men at the front carried spears and the two behind Serin carried the traditional short swords.

Serin herself was bound hand and foot and looked more weary than afraid. She was led into the middle of the room and I made way for her so that she could take my seat.

The High Priest tried one of his dreadful smiles.

"Good morning Serin. I am sorry we must meet under such unfortunate circumstances. It is not the intention of this court to prolong this matter further than may be necessary to establish the truth. Assss you are aware the Council has convened to consider the matters concerning yourself, the 'hill' and the 'sparrow'. I have spoken at length with the physician Bolanus about these disturbing occurrences and it is Bolanus' opinion you are not ill. More worrying perhaps he believes you to be telling the truth. This is a serious business that could have dire consequences for all of us. Before the Council reaches a decision, however, there are certain issues I would like you to clarify. Are you willing to speak to the Council?"

Serin looked up for the first time and shrugged her shoulders,

"It don't matter to me one way or other."

"Good, then can you tell me, are these voices talking to you at the moment?"

She shook her head.

"Serin. what do you think these spirits are trying to tell you?"

"If I knew that I wouldn't have spoken to old Ninias."

"You mussst have some opinion on the matter."

"I feel summat terrible is gonna happen in the woods by the river – summat involving kids."

"Our children?"

"No – I don't think so- Saxone kids maybe."

"Are you suggesting Cumbray will one day be in the hands of Saxones. Be careful how you answer. Some might consider such thoughts to be treason."

There was a flash of anger in her eyes,

"If you burn me for treason or black magic what difference does it make? You asked my opinion, I'm telling you I think children over there in the woods beside the river."

The High Priest called for silence with a wave of a talon-like hand as the ensuing clamour threatened to get out of control. He attempted another one of his ghastly smiles.

"I think I see. Someday there will be a great battle where the people of Cumbray will overcome the barbarian. Many Saxones will die – men, women, children."

"Maybe."

She didn't sound convinced.

"Why do you think, therefore, these heathen voices have spoken to you of all people?"

"That's what Ninias asked me. How would I know? Their words mean nothing to me. Perhaps it were the children's voices. I think they needed someone. They were frightened. I felt they needed me. There were this one particular little boy. He were lost and lonely. He wanted my help.""And the significance of the words 'hill' and 'sparrow'?"

"I've no idea. Ninias told me hill means mound. In one of the Saxone dreams I were on a grassy mound. I don't know meaning of other word."

"I can tell you it means small bird."

"Then it makes no sense to me."

The High Priest pursed half his lips

"Thank you Serin I have no further questions. You now have the opportunity to tell the Council anything else you feel we should know before we reach our decision. Have you anything further to say?"

"I suspect the Council's already made its mind up but I want everyone here to know I'm neither a traitor nor a witch. If I'm here to deliver a message to you from the Saxones why didn't they explain it to me."

She looked up at the assembly looking down on her and fluffed herself up.

"You can't wait to condemn me can you. Can't wait to burn me at stake for summat you don't understand. None on you has faintest idea what's going on here; not Dad, not Ninias, not the Women's court, none on you. You've no answer to all this so Serin must be a witch. Everything'll be alright once we get rid on witch. If it turns out later she were just mad well no harm done eh? It's only that pig man's daughter Serin we're talking about here. She can't have kids anyway so no loss. Well I tell you now it won't be alright. Killing me won't stop any on this.

Her eyes flitted around the silent court until she found me, " Dr. Bolanus – thank you at least for listening to my story. At least I'm grateful for that."

I nodded avoiding looking at her as they took her away.

The outcome was of course inevitable. Nonetheless there must have been some doubt in the minds of the Council because it took them two days to reach a verdict.I walked beside her as they lead her up execution hill. The whole village turned out but there wasn't the usual gaiety you see on such occasions. Everybody knew this was just something that needed to be done – like having to kill your prize egg-laying hen to avoid starvation. Even Serin seemed to accept the situation. She was just part of some drama of which she had little comprehension. Today was only the final inevitable outcome. She said nothing when they trussed her to the oak in the middle of the holy stone circle. The guards attempted to light the fire but the oak and holly branches were damp. Smoke billowed around the hill in acrid black clumps stinging the eyes and blocking out the light. I was watching Serin, waiting for the right moment to mercifully kill her. I had brought a sharpened spear in order to finish her off quickly. Even as the flames swept up beneath her she remained silent, staring in the direction of the river, as if looking for someone. I stepped towards her intending to use the spear. Then, in a reedy voice that makes my flesh creep even today, she began to sing.

In that moment I knew that the decision of the Council had been just. Her thin sharp voice echoed around the land like the mournful mew of a buzzard. She sang in a language I had never heard before and as her voice rose to the heavens I swear a host of invisible others joined in. I moved closer to the flames, raising my spear. As I looked into her face for the last time, to my astonishment, she was smiling.

**

Serin gathered the blonde Saxone boy lovingly to her breast. Others clung to her dress. All around her on the terraces the lost children of Hillsborough joined her in song.

"Walk on – Walk on – with hope in your heart and you'll never walk alone."

The Tapping on the Line

'**D**ek' has caught a frog in the long grass by the embankment; he grips it tightly in dirty cupped hands. Its tiny yellow head pokes out between his fingers. He calls out, "Found one Peg – it's a monster." He offers the little creature up for me to see. A sudden look of alarm crosses his face, "Watch out. I can't hold on to it. It's gonna jump." I fall backwards and he rolls on the ground laughing, gripping his sides as if the joke was painfully funny.

"You're dead scared you are – scared of a tinchy little frog."

"I'm not," I reply.

He circles the old brick well in the middle of the garden whooping, "Peggy Barnes – shit scared of a tinchy frog."

"I'm not – I'm not. And I'm telling Dad you swore."

He stops running and looks back down the Tramway cautiously as if Dad was about to appear.

"I never did."

"You did. You said S – H – I – T."

"That's not swearing." he says, but with little conviction, then smiles contritely, "You can stroke him if you like – he's not a pois-er-nous one."

"There's no such things as pois'nous frogs." I say but decline his invitation to approach. Dek grins, "Yes there is. For'ners die from eating them." He warms to the theme, "And in some countries they've got giant ones that even eat little girls."

We are distracted by a distant engine whistle from the direction of the City. It's the last tram of the day. There's only four trams on Sundays, and as usual I run to the end of the garden to watch it pass.

I love the Tram – the rattle of the coaches – the oily black smoke that stings your eyes – the way the ground shudders as the tired old engine trundles past our cottage.

Dek and I hang out like washing on the garden fence as the train goes by. I strain my eyes through the billow of smoke, trying to identify the ghostly figures I see in the cab; steamy shadows cast by the fire in the grate. Dad often rides the tram home at the end of his shift, jumping from the running plate when the train deliberately slows to allow him to alight. On this occasion, however, it passes without slowing. Dad must be away working further down the line. Tom Bennet, the fireman, waves manically to us as the three mismatched tired old coaches sway away from us like drunken men.

Dad's a trackman. Most days he's away somewhere doing some Mr. Fixit job or other. Our tramway is so run down these days he's always busy. When he's away us kids have to man the drawbridge. The drawbridge is really Dad's responsibility. An iron crude girder monstrosity, it was built by the Company to carry the tramway over the canal. When Dad's otherwise tied up it's our responsibility to work a hand winch and raise the bridge to let the increasingly rare coal barges through. The winch is on the far bank and we have to cross it to work the lift mechanism, Black waters slither beneath our feet, visible in the spaces between the cross girders. To most people the drawbridge doesn't look much but to us it's a gateway to an imaginary castle – I'm the princess and Dek the prince.

It's usually dark by the time Dad gets back. There are no trams after dark and Mam says, "Peggy – go see if your Dad's coming." I then open our garden gate and lie between the rails, my head on the cold metal. There's method in this madness. In the dark, Dad uses a stick, to feel for the rails and I listen for the familiar tapping on the line.

✶✶✶

"Curly's here." Mam's baking bread in our grey flag-stone kitchen, her big red arms pummelling the dough. Our fire spits and sparks in a boot-blacked hearth, while two dimpled loaves already prove on a tray by the fireside. She waves a powdery hand to the window, "Peggy, see to the winch for me – there's a good girl".

From the nearby towpath I also hear the splash of the bargee's old horse, Frankie, tramping through the muddy pools at the canal's edge. It's raining heavily and rainwater pours off Frankie's flanks like the chalk brooks on the distant Sussex Downs after a summer storm. The horse drags a filthy brown barge behind him that creaks and groans in time to his efforts. From the stern Curly Combes waves a coaly arm, "Hurry up Peggy – I'm drowning here." I step carefully along the wooden plank Dad has put between the sleepers on the bridge as a walkway. The rails shimmer and sparkle and below my feet the oily canal rolls and swirls dark, the viscous surface pitted with raindrops. Dek follows. We grab a winch handle each and pit our childish weight against resistant cogs and hawser. Imperceptibly at first, then with a metallic screech of reproach, the bridge slowly lifts and the coal barge slips past, its hold loaded to capacity with the twinkling black jewels that fuel the gas lamps of the city.

Dek is stood on cross struts at the top of the raised bridge, waving to the boat as it slips away into the mist and rain. He clambers down and together we lower the bridge. It is then I hear the tapping on the rails and I turn and run down the slippery trackway into my father's arms.

"How's my favourite girl?" he says.

His jacket is soaked through, pungent with the smell of oil and sulphur. I cling to his neck, hands clasped behind his head. Dad also picks up my brother and carries him piggy-back to the cottage. Dek takes Dad's stick, as always, as we gingerly cross back over the canal bridge. Dad's face brushes my neck.

"Your chin's all prickly Daddy. You're all wet."

He laughs, making to rub his sandpaper stubble against my cheek. We step down into the kitchen of the cottage sprinkling the weather on to the stone floor.

"Something smells good.", Dad says. My parents hug.

"Water's boiled – you can wash for tea."

Mum fills an old pewter bowl and hangs a towel by the fire to warm. "Where were yer today?"

He reaches for the towel, spluttering suds like the spits of condensed steam from the Tram engine.

Mam grimaces, "You never went down to the village?"

"I work where they send me Betty, you know that."

She looks away, "Any news?"

He hesitates, looking sadly across at me, "A girl about Peg's age. yesterday. They reckon it's touch and go with her mum 'n' all."

"What is it now?"

"I don't know – more'n twenty mebbes. Kids, old folks. Curly says they've a special ward for 'em at the City."

"Keep away from the village Jack. They say the air's sour down there." She pulls me into the folds of her skirt.

He shrugs , "I work where they send me."

***

The following day I am sat playing with my dolls on the kitchen floor.

There is a tentative knock at the door and it's Tom Bennet. He wheezes steam in the cold winter air, fingering a ragged cap he holds tightly against his stomach.

"'Scuse me for comin', Missus but I heard how there's been an accident with the Tram near the village. Some folks hurt – don't know how many. Last train jumped the rails and slid down into the marsh."

"Jack…Was Jack?"

"S'all I know Missus."

"I'll get down there…see if."

"Best not, I'd say Missus – stay here with the kids – there's nothing you can do anyway and it'll soon be dark. The Company's running a special up from the City to get the injured to the infirm'ry."

Later. I weep into my pillow. Dek whispers across the room, "Peg – Peggy".

"Don't cry Pegs, Dad'll be awright. You'll see."

He gets out of his bed. He has not undressed.

"Where yer goin'?" I ask.

"Down the track to look for Dad."

"I'm comin' with yer." He shakes his head, glancing towards the light from under our parent's bedroom door.

"I want to come Dek. Please?"

He bites his lip, "Be quiet then or Mum'll hear us."

I slip a jacket over my nightdress and pull on my heavy boots. We slip quietly down the stairs. Dek liftd the latch and we step out into the sharp frosty night. The cold hits you like the biting shock of the sea on sunburnt skin. A full moon is shining through thin cloud, looking to my eyes like the headlamp of a Tram locomotive engulfed in steam. We drop down the embankment next to our garden onto the track. The rainy rails now lead the way.

We step from sleeper to sleeper. Through our own sleeping rural halt with its lonely corrugated metal shelter. Past the hulk of an abandoned geriatric locomotive in a siding. Past a line of decaying trucks and then out into the whispering darkness of the countryside.

✶✶✶

Hours pass.

I no longer feel tired or cold – just numb. Time is measured by the rhythm of footfall on wooden sleeper. We are a train. Dek is the Tram engine and I the guards van.

It starts to get light.

I can now see the horizon, a band of blue on black. Around me the mysterious silhouette of hedge. The fields next to the rails are studded with the glowing eyes of invisible animals who watch us pass.

Is that the sea in the distance? The rails here run along the sea wall. The sighing ocean off to our left. On our right are wild tidal rills and marram stubbled marsh; in front of us I can see an ominous crackling glow.

"You smell out Peggy?"

I nod. I had also noticed the acrid burning smell.

Abruptly the rail to our right separates from the sleepers and loops down the embankment into the saltmarsh.

And then there it is, the Tramway company's old saddle-tank engine, nose down, in the mud, an ancient ex-works engine that should have been scrapped years ago. The smokebox door has sheered from the boiler exposing rows of weeping steam pipes. The boiler is skewed to one side and the long stovepipe chimney has fallen to one side and is now half buried in the mud. Steam creeps from a horizontal split in the boiler. There are no signs of passengers or crew. Behind the locomotive the leading coach has ridden up over the intervening buffers crushing the cab. A second coach stands incongruously on its end; towering in the centre of the wreckage, frozen in mid-cartwheel by the coach behind which has concertinaed into the rear. At the tail end of the debris an undamaged guards van hangs half on and half off the track. The rotting remains of what was had been a train full of happy holidaymakers heading for the beach groans in the freshening sea breeze.

It is Dek who makes the first move – running down the embankment to sink up to his knees in the clinging mud of the saltmarsh. He wades through the quagmire towards the train and I aim to follow him when I hear a wonderful sound,

"Peggy – wait."

★ ★ ★

It was strange for the library to be open late. Close inspection revealed a light on only in a cramped office behind the checkout desk. The man from the Record Office stopped the tape momentarily as the old lady gathered her thoughts,

"Dad was in the first work party sent to clear the area before the heavy cranes and cutting gear were brought in, you see. He told Mum the fireman was killed instantly. The coaches were full of schoolkids – poor bairns. There were loads in the papers after the enquiry. They said it was an 'unavoidable accident' – an 'act of God' like, but Dad had known those sleepers were rotten and he blamed himself. That was why, for a few weeks, he gave up his spare time to help up at the hospital; just fetchin' and carryin' like. Anything he could do for them what had been hurt. He had no reason to feel guilty like that. It was the Company's fault. They spent hardly anything on track maintenance. That was where Dad caught the diphtheria, I suppose, from those people from the village on that special ward. Before long we'd all caught it. It wasn't like it is now. Lots of people died from it back then and our Derek was really poorly. I remember Dad running to the hospital down the tramway in the pouring rain, with Dek in his arms. There were no buses or trams after dark, so he had to run all that way to the city poor man.

He came home a couple of nights later. I was playing by the side of the Tramway when I heard the familiar tapping on the line. Dad couldn't use his stick, you see, if he was carrying our Derek so I knew straight away like. He was alone.

Jaguar and Panther

Jaguar arrived this weekend. He came, as usual, by taxi; his woollen muffler wound tightly around the lower part of his face to mask his features. Strolling into the house without knocking, he nodded to me in passing, and took up his usual position with his backside to the fire. Tony was anticipating his arrival and ran down the stairs to greet him and was dutifully made a fuss of. After kissing me routinely on the cheek father and son retired to the garden where they played ball games until it was too dark to see. So it was not until later when we had all eaten and Anthony had been put to bed that I got chance to talk to him alone. He was rummaging in his valise for his notebook.

"How was your journey?" I asked.

"Same as ever." He said without looking up.

"And the Reform Club?"

'Huh', he snorted.

"Did any of your friends mention my book by any chance?" I asked, knowing that there was unlikely to have been no comments, given its popular notoriety.

Jaguar shook his head and growled.

"What did you think of it?" I asked.

He stopped scribbling in his notebook and looked up, "What?'

"My book. You've read it. What did you make of it?".

He gave me a look that implied he hadn't time for such trivia,

"Do you really want to know?"

"Of course. Your honest opinion please."

There was a long silence while he thought this through,

"My honest opinion?" he hesitated, "Well, your work continues to show – er -promise." He began, "There are flaws, obvious flaws, but nevertheless promise – some promise." He turned back to the fire and continued making notes.

"What flaws?" I asked.

"Look I'm very busy. I've a very important article to write for the Times with a Thursday deadline and…"

"What flaws?" I persisted.

Those grey eyes I had loved so much flashed angrily,

"You want an honest opinion? Well if you must know. I've seen better – even from you. How can I put this without hurting your feelings? 'The Judge', my dear Panther, 'The Judge' is a ugly sprawl of a book with a faked hero and faked climax. *That* is my honest opinion."

He turned his back on me again to indicate that the discussion was over.

"Thank you. You're too kind as always," I replied as I walked out of the room. I was clearing the dinner plates from the dining room table when I felt his hand on my shoulder.

"I can see I've upset you Panther dear. That was not my intention," he said soothingly. "As I said your work shows promise. I only adversely criticise because I know you are capable of so much more." He turned me round and gave me the briefest of hugs, that felt more of a businessman's handshake than an embrace from a lover.

"There now. No need for tears. When was the last time a panther cried? It's of no importance. Nothing of consequence. Why do you still feel this odd compulsion for this silly 'hobby' of yours anyway? You're financially sound. You have the cottage and the boy and…"

"And what?" I asked, "What else have I got? Living out here in the middle of nowhere I no longer see any of my friends. There are no entertainments, no theatres, no picture houses. The village even has only one shop. The only stimulation my poor brain gets is from my writing. I would have thought that you of all people would understand that. And what about you? Your life revolves around London. You come home less and less. It doesn't seem that long since you told me you couldn't bear to live a moment without me."

He looked up,

"Have I not provided a good home for you and the boy?"

"You have." I acknowledged.

"Then what?" he demanded irritably.

"There has to be more – much more. What happened to the great love we had? We were once two halves of the same person. We thought alike. We fought the world side by side. Jaguar and Panther together."

He leaned back in the armchair, his hands behind his head, staring into the fire. Whole minutes passed.

"I suppose now is as good a time as any to tell you."

"Tell me what," I asked suspecting the answer before he spoke.

"The truth is I've found someone else. I'm in love with someone else." His voice betrayed no emotion. It was like he was giving one of his lectures on 'things to come'.

"Who is it," I asked trying to keep my voice steady.

"Do you really want to know?" he replied.

I nodded.

"It's someone I've known and worked with for many years. I'd always considered her just a friend until now but we were thrown together for a few weeks during my recent lecture tour. She helped me out – helped me out a lot. Attended to me when I was too tired to perform. Typed up my notes…"

"Do I know her?," I asked, my hands shaking.

He nodded, "It's Jane," he said simply.

Anger welled up in my breast, "You're giving up your family after all these years for Jane? Plain Jane? You always said you couldn't stand the sight of her."

He shrugged,

"I never meant it to happen. Sometimes love just develops even with someone you've known for years."

Tears filled my eyes as he stood up,

"I suppose I'd better go then", he said, "Tell Anthony I'll make arrangements to see him sometime next month. He won't want for anything you know that Rebecca."

It was the first time he had used my real name since the first day we'd met.

"Oh go. For God's sake go", I replied, "Go back to your plain Jane."

I watched from the bedroom window as he walked down the garden path for the last time his muffler bound tightly round his face. He would never need to be an invisible man again. Herbert George Wells was going home to his wife.

Your Friendly Neighbourhood Club Man
(*With an appreciative nod to Chaucer's 'Friars Tale'*)

There's only one streetlamp. I park beneath it, double check the car doors, walk a few yards down the road then go back and check the doors again. It's that sort of neighbourhood. I do good business round here.

"Club Man," I bang hard on the door so she'll hear over Coronation Street.

Try again. This time louder.

The passage light comes on and there's a scrabble of assorted unboltings and unlatchings before the door fractionally opens.

"Club Man missus."

One eye and a lank of grey hair flickers at the edge of the door, "Is that you Jack?"

"Aye – let's in Betty. A'm freezing out here."

I brush past her and take up residence in the padded armchair in front of the fire

"Make us a cuppa will you Bet a'm nithered."

She disappears into the kitchen returning, before I'm properly warmed through, bearing a cheap china teapot and two mismatched cups and saucers.

"Joe down the Social?" I ask.

She nods.

"How's his back these days?"

"Has his good and bad days," she replies.

"What is it this week Jack?" She offers me a biscuit from a large square tin with a photo of salubrious Seaton Carew on the lid.

"Six weeks Betty."

"Six weeks – never is – *Six weeks?*"

"Aye six weeks – and the last time you never paid nowt off the back. I can't let it go again this week – more than me job's worth."

"What's it come to now then pet?"

"It's eighteen bob, counting this one."

She's lost her specs as usual and screws her eyes up as she counts out coins from an old black purse she keeps in her pinafore pocket.

"I could manage two shillin' a suppose.".

"It'll have to be more than two bob this week Betty. If it were down to me , but you know what they're like down the shop." I take the purse from her hand, "Is that a ten bob note?".

She tries to take it back. For a wrinkly she can certainly move fast when she wants to.

"Yer can't take all that Jack. It's all a've got 'til pension day."

" A'm sorry pet, even with this yer still two weeks in arrears." She can really lay it on this one.

"Yer can't take ten shillin'. Not ten shillin." There's waterworks on the way.

"Now Betty no need to get yourself all upset". I dump the rest of the contents of her scabby purse into her open palm. " A've not took it all". "Your trouble is yer will keep buying stuff off us yer can't afford." I sit down and sip my tea which, because of the whingeing, is gettingt cold.

"Give us yer 'payin' in' book Betty and a'll bring it up to date."

The tears flow in earnest now.

Time for the sales pitch.

"Have you thought about a new frock for Easter Bet? Give yer old man a thrill. The new catalogue's just out. Or stays? A new set of them wouldn't go amiss by the looks of it and yer won't even have to increase yer weekly payment.

She ignores me but I leave the catalogue anyway, drink up, and let myself out.

★★★

I go back to the car and check the doors again. Some kid's kicking a ball around under the light from the lamp. "Mind yer car mister?" Money grubbing little bastard'll get nowt from me.

Couple more calls and I'm finished. Don't push meself too hard on a Friday. Never know when you might need that extra bit of 'umph' – if you get my drift.

The lights are on at number 10. I check the tally book. Kitty Welford. Young Alan's first week at the high school if I'm not mistaken. Kitty opens the door. Seems in no hurry to let me in. Christ but she's looking clapped out these days. All skin and bone and a wheeze on her like a leaking valve. One too many 'Woodies' with this lady methinks.

"It's far too dear your stuff Jack, ". Her arms are folded in the 'No' position, " I can't afford owt from your Club."

"It's your decision Kitty. I'd be the last person to tempt anyone to spend beyond their means but you know how snotty these grammar school kids can be. Ever heard of intellectual snobbery?"

"No but if you're selling it I don't want it, " she smiles sourly.

Miserable cow. I check the car again but the kid has moved away.

✶✶✶

Number 12's interesting. Got a garden. Yes I did say garden. The real sort with flowers and a lawn. Most of the houses round here don't have lawns. Just glorified litter trays for their dogs to shit in. The occupants are a young copper and his misses. Now what do I know about the boys in blue? They're all freemasons? Now there's a club worth belonging to.

"Club Man." I ring the doorbell. It works! A working doorbell in this street – amazing! The door's opened by this bruiser with a crew-cut. He's in his shirt sleeves and there's splashes of paint on his bare arms.

"Yeah?"

"Sorry to bother you. I can see yer busy."

"What do you want?" He isn't pleased to see me. His accent suggests he's from somewhere south of Leeds.

"I'm the Club Man – from 'Deacons'. You know. Clothing clubs like." I produce my ID card, which he scrutinises suspiciously.

"Carol," he calls out, "You been buying stuff from Deacons?"

Carol's at the back of the house, "You know I did pet. I got that suit I wore the other night at the French's party –

and the blue dress with the matching shoes I wore at Bridget's wake."

P.C. Plod gives me a look that suggests he'd be happy to catch me resisting arrest, "You better come in then."

I follow him into the living room where all the furniture's hidden beneath paint covers. There's a couple of step-ladders linked by a plank running the length of the room. The ceiling's in the process of turning a pukey mauve colour.

"Beautiful", I tell him, "lovely colour purple."

"Carol get yourself out here," the purple speckled police-man addresses the kitchen.

Some tart in her early twenties, hair wrapped in a towel, sticks her head round the door,

"Can yer pay him for us pet? A'm in me knickers here." She looks me up and down, "The poor man doesn't want to see me with no clothes on now does he?"

"How much does she owe then?" He wipes his hands on one of the paint sheets and starts fishing through the pockets of a coat hung on a peg behind the kitchen door.

"Just two weeks ", I use my apologetic voice, "Six and fourpence. Your wife's owes four bob on one book and two and four on the other. If it's awkward – I can see you're decorating – I can always come back next week."

"She thinks I'm made of money."

"That's what they're like", I sympathise, trying to start a conversation, "You're not from round here right?"

"No," he replies.

"But your lass is a local if ah'm not mistaken?"

He doesn't have the courtesy to reply, so I try another approach.

"Just between you and me you'd be better off getting this stuff from Marks and Sparks. Our stuff's overpriced for what it is."

"You've no need to tell me that." he snaps back.

I can see my Masonic apron disappearing before my eyes.

"Same time again next week?", I say pleasantly.

He ushers me to the door.

Some people are just pig ignorant.

∗ ∗ ∗

My final call is number 35 – as always.

I tap on the door and the curtains open slightly.

"That you Jack?"

"Open up Pauline It's cold as a penguins chuff out here."

"Door's on the latch. Let yerself in"

She's stood by the window with little Sandra in her arms. Good looking piece Pauline.

Bodywork in good nick with long brown hair and a pretty, if slightly worn, face. The twins Karen and Peter are playing on the uncovered stone floor. She lays the child she is carrying down gently in its pram and covers her with a thin blanket. The room stinks as-per-usual. Place is the same every time I come here. Kid's filthy, room filthy. The only items in the room not filthy are all the 'Hail Mary' stuff. Walls covered in portraits of unidentified saints and the baby Jesus. She's even got a huge jewelled cross over the fireplace, must have cost a fortune, and there's all her kids running around with no arses to their pants.

How can anyone live like this? I could understand it if she were some slag off the estate but Pauline's educated, classy. She should have more self-respect. Trouble is she married that wanker Ken Vasey, who's several chips short of a fish supper if you ask me. I can only think he turned her head with his bluff northern manner, rough navvy hands and flat working cap.

As expected of all good Catholics the kids arrived almost immediately. And now here she is. Living in this rathole. Second hand furnishings. A sideboard that looks like it's cobbled together from old fish boxes. Lumpy armchair, arms tattooed with ciggie burns and sprawled across it their smelly Labrador dog Butch. He looks up and starts wagging his tail as I enter the room. In the corner the television, the only new furniture in the room, blasts away to its disinterested doggy audience.

"Cup of tea Jack?" I nod. The weekend starts here.

"Milk but no sugar. A'm sweet enough as it is." She manages a weak smile and heads off into the kitchen. I brush the dog off the chair and sit down, warming me hands in front of the fire.

I reach across and switch the telly off calling out, "Yer weren't watching this were yer pet?".

I check her account. Here it is – Pauline Vasey – nicely in arrears.

When was the last time she paid anything? Three months ago? Yes and then all the arrears mysteriously cleared in one go. Well settlement time's come round again.

She re-enters the room carrying a tray with two battered pewter mugs and a teapot with no lid.

She's loosened her hair so it swings seductively from side to side as she walks.

"Here you are Jack. You like it nice and strong don't you?"

She knows how I like it.

I tap me ledger forcefully, "Bit behind our Pauline. Said nothing 'til now but they'll be asking questions back at the shop if yer don't settle up soon."

"How much is it?" she asks in that silky voice that always gets me bits going.

"Eleven weeks a'm afraid pet. They never let it go beyond three months". I try to look concerned.

"You know how it is as well as I do Jack. Yard's laid off most of the men. Ken's luckier than most. At least he's in work even if it's only maintenance stuff. But you know he only gets the bare wage."

Action time.

"Sorry Pauline love but I've got to take something off the arrears this week or a'm in deep shit mesel."

I drain the cup and stand up. Fortunately, Pauline knows the score. She's not daft, I'll say that for her, "Sadly Jack I've nothing for you … unless."

"Unless what Pauline love?" It's times like this I *really* love my job. "Ken still on nights is he?"

She nods.

"Well then Ah'm sure we can work something out. We usually do."

***

Two happy hours later and it's back to the car. Thorough check round. Having refused to support that little yob's protection racket you can never be too sure.

There's chalk scrawled on the pavement:

'Revench of the Feend from Hell'

Bollocks. Go round, check the car again. Nothing obviously wrong though. Tyres OK, bodywork OK, no graffito:

Headlights, wing mirrors, fine. Get out while the goings good. I hit the accelerator and roar down towards the lights at the bottom of the hill, smiling to myself. 'Revench of the Feend from Hell' indeed. The lights change to red and as I brake hard there's this scream of metal on stone and sparks billow out from each side of the bonnet. My final thought. Of course, I didn't check the wheel nuts.

The car, minus front wheels, slides gracefully out into the fast-flowing stream of traffic.

Saturday Matinee

It's my turn to pay so it costs me nowt to get in. Stew goes round collecting the money.

"Me Mam never girrus owt this week," That was 'Army' trying it again. He turns the pockets of his anorak inside out to show us they're empty.

"Yer always say that. What's in yer trousers?" Stew grabs his belt but Army twists away and runs off. Stew chases him and twists his arm up his back 'til he shells out.

"Yer bastard that was all I had for the week."

"Yerra lying get. Yer Gran gets her pension on a Thursday."

"Mebbes – but she never gives me owt."

"Well nick summat out her purse, she's doolally anyway. It's not like she'll miss it."

"She's not as daft as yer'd think. She caught me last week and told Mam. Dad beat the shit out of us when he got home."

"Do yer want to go or don't yer?"

Stew makes as if he's going to hand back the twopence he's taken but Army just shrugs and looks away.

"Right – anyone else not coming?" No answer.

Stew takes off his dut and holds it out for the rest to put money into. They all pay up except for that cow Patty Hamilton who puts nothing in, same as usual. She gives him that smarmy smile,

"Ah'm really short this week Stew pet. Could yer put it in forrus and I'll pay yer Tuesday – else I won't be able to go?"

It's not fair. Why does she always gerroff without paying? Just because she's got big tits – makes me sick. She's nothing else to offer. Brain the size of a ball bearing and her arse hanging out of those raggy jeans she got off her brother. You won't believe, but she has this really Bazpid pony tail, which she thinks makes her look like Doris Day in Calamity Jane. She swings her head about all the time so you notice it more – AND – she's got a Bazpid piggy nose like a pekinese dog. Cow. Me Mam says 'She'll end up just like her mother that one – on the bloody streets'.

"Ple-e-e-a-se Stew darling." She squeezes her lips together like Marilyn Monroe in that film 'Some Like it Hot' and Stew sinks into his jacket, red in the face.

"Right – just this once. You berra remember it next week," he says but we all know she'll pull the same trick next Sat'day.

Stew never pays for me to get in.

He hands over the money. Nine pence in ha'pennies and pennies. We could get in the 'Plad' for sixpence but then we'd have to go downstairs. You need a tin hat down there. Better be a 'thrower' than a 'thrown upon' I always say.

When was the last time yer went to the Plad? It used to be one of the best picture houses in the town me Mam said. Back in the days when it was called The Palladium – when they had a proper doorman with one of those posh jackets who was called the Admiral on account on his fancy uniform with lapels. You had to get there early in those days to get a seat, and they wouldn't let kids into 'X' films. You had to be eighteen. Queuing right down the street then, even for those crappy English films in black and white. The Admiral would come out and shout 'Two seats in the '1 and 10's and all the grownups would look around to see who was there with no kids.

Families were usually split up. You could either go in separately during the 'B' feature or wait for the first house to turn out when you might get four or five seats together if you were lucky. All I remember of them days is standing outside for hours queuing in the pouring rain.

Nowadays you can sit most anywhere you like but no grownups bother much. The new cinemas in the town centre have taken all the Plad's trade away. All you ever get during the week, now anyway, is repeats.

Saturday's different though.

On Saturday morning's the Plad's pretty full, and getting fuller since they started doing the 'specials'.

Even so, I heard the 'specials' started as a mistake.

I've been coming to the Saturday matinees since I was old enough to come on me own – four or five I must have been, and through the years the place has slowly emptied. Sad really but that's how it is. I'll probably keep coming 'til they close the place down. It's the cowboy films see. I've always loved them. They're great. All those big fellers with American accents and guns; Dale Robertson, Audie Murphy, Roy Rogers; even Bill Boyd, or Hopalong Cassidy to you – though he does have those funny piggy eyes that put me off. Matinees are the best. You get loads for your money. There's a main feature, often a cowboy but sometimes a gangster, a couple of cartoons and a serial, and that's often a cowboy as well. Anyway, where was I? Oh yeah – the specials. What happened, Stew told me, is that one Saturday someone mixed up the boxes and instead of the cowboy film they started showing an 'X' which they normally show after the pubs shut. It was the ice cream lady who spotted what was happening, 'cos all the lads were cheering. It's beyond me. Given the choice I'd have the cowboy anytime rather than some dirty film about a silly holiday camp where everyone goes around starkers, but the lads loved it and word got round even though they only showed twenty minutes of the nudie film before it was stopped.

The Plad was packed the following week but they didn't make the same mistake again and the week after that, of course, they were back to the same few regulars like me. Naturally they tried the same trick again a couple of weeks later with same result. Following week – place packed out. Since then it's been a regular thing. Not every week like. Just enough to keep the big lads coming but with enough gaps so they could pretend the tits and bums are genuine mistakes.

Like I said, I prefer the cowboy films but I know Stew, Army, Col and Baz are just as bad as the rest when it comes to some fat woman flapping her whatsits about. Anyway, about the scam.

Seven of us wait over the road from the Plad; Stewart (Stew) Mitchell, David (Army) Armstrong, Barry (Baz) Patterson, Colin (Col) Teesdale, Patty Hamilton, her little sister Rita and me. Patty's sister's only six but Patty drags her round with her all the time. Colin's older than us but a bit thick, Baz's in Stews class. He never says much. His Mam cuts his hair so it looks awful. A ragged fringe. His clothes are old fashioned too. Just like Stew, Col and Army wear drainpipes and winkle pickers but Baz wears the sort of stuff you only get out of women's magazines; Fair Isle jumpers, plastic, round toed, shoes and respectable looking trousers with a sharp crease down the front.

Saturday Matinee

I pocket the entrance money and join the queue to get in. This consists of mostly lads these days, trying to grab the seats in front stalls to get as close as possible to the screen and its six foot bazookas.

"Stalls or upper circle?", says Doreen.

"Upper circle Doreen please," I reply.

"Nine pence", says Doreen, "and ah'm not Doreen to you."

She wears a badge with 'Doreen' on it.

The lads behind me are sniggering.

"Six for the stalls Doreen dearest", says one.

There's a queue for the sweet counter but I've no spare money for sweets so go straight upstairs. Picture houses, even the run-down ones like the Plad are really posh aren't they? They've got thick carpets on the floors – not just rag mats like home – and photos of old film stars on the walls. Amongst the signed photos (if you can believe it) are pictures of people like Gene Kelly and Bob Hope. There's even one enormous picture of some owld gadgee called Wilfrid Hyde White, smiling and shaking hands with the Plad manager, from those far-off days when the Plad was popular. I don't know who Wilfrid Hyde White is but I'm guessing he never got into a shootout with John Wayne.

The lady with the torch shows me to my seat. There's no need really because the film hasn't started and the lights are all on. I think she just does it for something to do. She'd be better spending her time stopping the pitched battle in the front circle. There's kids climbing over seats, kids fighting in the aisles, shouting, crying, beating each other up. I reckon it's the beer ice lollies. What's your opinion on *them*? To me they taste horrible but the big lads feel they've got to buy them to look good in front of their mates. It's not right is it – selling beer to kids? Even if they do stick a bit of apple in to make them look more respectable. It's as bad as selling tabs to kids. They shouldn't do that either – but they do.

Luckily I'm in the rear circle which is a bit quieter and there's less chance of getting hit by flying ice. That's the trouble with beer lollies, once you've sucked the beer out of them all they're good for is throwing. Anyway, just when it looks like the fighting's getting out of hand, the main lights go down and a spotlight lights up the centre of the stage where Fatty Fletcher, the cinema manager, appears from behind the curtain. It's the same patter every week,

"Hi kids."

Some general booing

"I said HI KIDS"

Some 'Hi Fatty's' but even more booing including a loud voice from the stalls, "Gerroff you fat get."

Fatty never gets the message though. He carries on like he's the main feature,

"What's it to be this week?"

This used to always get the little'uns shouting 'CARTOONS' but it just shows how times have changed because it's now the big lads who shout back,

"Something for the boys Fatty."

Fatty smirks and puts one hand to his lughole,

"What's that, I didn't hear yer?"

"SOMETHING FOR THE LADS FATTY"

The curtain starts to draw back and, as he turns to go, he calls out,

"Well we'll just have to see won't we."

A shower of beery ice follows him off the stage.

As the lights dim Bugs Bunny appears on the screen to a big cheer. Bugs is my favourite. 'Whats up Doc?' You know. All that stuff.

I would have liked to stay and watch but instead I make my way towards the greenlit 'Exit' sign as if I'm going to the bog. There's no-one around so I nip down the stairs and open the emergency doors using them funny metal bar things you lean on. The others are outside. Patsy complains as usual,

"What yer been doing 'til now? Bloody freezing out here."

"You shut up", I say,"else I'll tell them yer gorrin without paying."

She gives me one of her stuck up looks and pushes past me, dragging her sister off to the loo to wait 'til it's all clear. The lads head for the gents and I return to my seat. Over the next half hour, one by one, they slip in, until the seats around me are filled up.

Everyone's in by the time the main feature comes on. It's 'Roy Rogers and the Indian Uprising'. Half the audience, including me, gets up and cheers. It's in black and white though which is an excuse for Stew and Army to try being funny.

Stew stands on his seat,

"I-N-D-I-A-N-S "

Then all the lads along the row do that stupid trick where you sit down hard on your seat, sending up puffs of dust like smoke signals.

The film though's really good. Some gold prospectors have been digging in Indian territory and have started an Indian war. Roy Rogers goes and pow-wows with the chief. If he can get the white men off the Indian's land he can stop the war. As he rides back these bad guys ambush him and he falls off Trigger over a cliff edge. Just when it's all getting exciting the worst thing possible happens. Roy Rogers disappears and some fat women appear, tits out, throwing a beach ball to each other to loud cheers from the lads. Stew's straight away up on his seat punching the air, followed by Army who just does what Stew does. All the lads in the row are either standing on their seats or, if tall, like Col, are just standing up to see better.

"Why's that lady got no clothes on?", asks Rita.

"She's on her holidays." says her sister.

"Why's she got a hairy tummy?" says Rita.

"That's not hair, that's her swimming cossy." says Patsy, but I swear Rita knows she's lying.

Suddenly Roy Rogers is back on the screen again, to loud boos from the lads. That's all the lads ever get, a quick flash of tits, a beach ball and some bare bums.

Patsy turns to Stew,

"I look better than that."

"Show us then," says Stew.

"I might and I mightn't.", she replies.

The cow.

I turn away.

Baz has remained seated, waiting for the cowboy film to restart.

He sees me looking at him.

"I've seen this before," he says, "Roy lands on a ledge and Trigger rescues him."

He's right. There's this narrow ledge, just below the top of the cliff, and Roy manages to grab it as he's falling. He calls out to Trigger and the horse looks over the cliff top.

"The lasso Trigger", he calls out, "Get the lasso".

Trigger undoes the rope from the saddle with his teeth and lowers one end to Roy who grabs it. Trigger walks backward and pulls Roy all the way up to the top. I've seen Trigger do this sort of thing loads of times. He's really clever.

That's the best bit in the film though, apart from this shoot out with the gold miners. There's three of them with guns and Roy only has three bullets left but he still manages to shoot the guns out of their hands and knock all the baddies out just as the sheriff and the posse arrive.

The film ends and the lights go up. Stew goes around asking us all for more money to buy tabs. Between us we've only got enough to buy a couple of 'woodies'.

Army goes off to get the tabs from the ice cream lady.

We're not supposed to smoke in the cinema but everyone does and nobody says anything.

Stew lights up, takes a drag and passes the tab around. That cow Patty hangs on to it 'til we all moan. Rita isn't allowed to smoke. I don't think it's right, smoking at six, anyway.

I offer the tab to Baz.

"No thanks," he says.

"Why not?" I ask.

"They make me cough. I'm an asthmatic."

"What's that mean?" He looks alright to me.

"I get short of breath."

I pass the woodie back to Army.

"They're bad for you." I tell him and Baz smiles. I hadn't thought about it, what with his Fair Isle jumper and everything, but he has a sweet smile.

"Do you like cowboy fillums then?" I ask.

"Love them. Have you ever seen 'She Wore a Yellow Ribbon'? It's a cavalry one with John Wayne in it."

"No," I reply," Is it good?" "Good? It's fantastic. Loads of red Indians. It's in colour as well."

Baz knows lots about films. He's even got into some 'A' cert ones such as 'Shane' which I couldn't see. We get chatting about which is the best cowboy film ever. My favourite is 'Gunfight at the OK Corral' but Baz has this great list of John Wayne's. Just before the lights dim again he pulls a bag of sweets from his pocket.

"Liquorice allsorts." he says, holding the bag open.

I never noticed this before but he has lovely eyes.

The Wreck of the Hesperus

To those assembled in the office of the Hundred of Manhood and Selsey Tramway the news was greeted with something approaching hostility.

"The thing is," said Driver Blackettt, "the men all feel it would be better if His Majesty came by coach."

"Nonsense," said Colonel Stephens, twisting the end of his waxed moustache with annoyance. "The King will have travelled all the way from Balmoral – some five hundred miles. We can't expect him to get off the royal train at Chichester just to complete the last eight miles by coach when there's a perfectly serviceable railway ready and available for His Highness to use."

There was some shuffling of feet before Blackettt spoke up again,

"Truth is Colonel it 'ud look far worse if King's train broke down somewheres 'tween here and City – 'specially when er's come all that way."

The immaculately maintained moustache of Lieutenant Colonel Holman Stephens, Engineer and M.D. of the Tramway bristled, 'There will never be a better time, Blackettt, to laud the virtues of the Tram. Just imagine, gentlemen, the prestige a little railway such as ours might gain simply by simply displaying a 'By Appointment' crest'".

Some of the assembled railwaymen turned involuntarily to glance through the office window towards the ragbag of mismatched, cast off and condemned engines rusting away in the marshalling yard.

"Truth is Colonel we've only the one working loco – 'er 'Hesperus' – and she were old when the King's grandmother were on the throne."

After a slight hesitation Holman Stephens replied, "Hesperus is a splendid locomotive. She just needs a little – attention".

"What 'er needs, if you don't mind me saying Colonel, is a new boiler", interjected fireman Barnes," She can't hold 'er steam. She's more holes in 'er than…, " he looked around for a suitable simile, "than these overalls. This morning, f'rinstance, we had to wait for an hour below Kipson Bank to get enough steam just to haul two coaches over the hill, and them half empty. A bloody hour. The whole journey from Chichester's only supposed to take half an hour."

The Colonel reddened,

"His Highness is coming to Chichester Thursday week for the racing at Goodwood, after which, at 1830 hours precisely, he is going to board the Royal Train for an official reception and banquet at the Marine Hotel, Selsey. From Chichester, His Highness's Royal Train is going to be pulled by one of our engines and the King will be greeted at Selsey Town Station by myself and the Town Mayor. From there", he continued, "an open carriage will convey the Royal party onward. There are no 'ifs' and 'buts' gentlemen. That is what will happen." He emphasised each point by rapping hard on the desktop with the end of a pencil, which subsequently broke in two. "You have one week to prepare. I want to see baskets of flowers on all the station platforms and all employees are to wear the official Company uniform, pressed and clean…"

The Superintendent coughed.

"Hallet?" said Holman Stephens.

"If you remember Colonel you told us uniforms was just for the station masters. As I recall you said uniforms for manuals were 'an unnecessary expense for a Light Railway'."

"Mmm,," the Colonel's fingers returned to his moustache, "In which case," he decided," all station masters between here and Chichester will donate their uniforms, on the day, to the memebers of staff working at both the terminus stations. New overalls will however", he added generously, "be purchased for the driver and fireman of the Hesperus. Hesperus will also be provided with a fresh coat of paint for the occasion." He paused momentarily before adding. "A back-up engine will, of course, be maintained in steam in the unlikely event that there is an unforeseen problem with Hesperus. Hallet, if I may, I will now inspect the rolling stock." He marched off military style, head held high, in the direction of the engine sheds, leaving his Superintendent fuming.

The shed was a short walk from the station along a trackbed replete with thistles and long grass. As they approached the dilapidated wooden building two dirty children ran out past him clutching stolen booty.

"Them little buggers's nicking our eggs Jack," said permanent way man Glyn (Taffy) Tapholme and before Stephens knew what was happening Taffy, and Railway Carpenter Jack Miller, ran off in wheezing pursuit. The Colonel turned to Hallet,

"What does he mean 'nicking our eggs'?"

Stephen's deputy squirmed,

"Well you see… It's like this Colonel… I might have said it was alright to keep a few hens in the shed on account as it weren't likely as old 'Ringing Rock'' would ever be back in steam and old 'Morous' is now only good for parts."

The Colonel pushed his Superintendent angrily aside. It was dark inside the shed, the only light a shaft of sunlight lancing through the dusty air from a ragged hole in the roof. Large pieces of unidentified machinery, presumably from the ill-fated Morous, littered the two tracks, one of which was occupied by Ringing Rock.

It was not in good condition.

This, the most recent engine purchased by the 'Hundred of Manhood and Selsey Tramway', looked beyond repair. Its smoke box door hung precariously from one hinge displaying, like rows of rotting teeth, a line of protruding steam pipes. The rest of the locomotive fared no better. Its once gleaming boiler was now the drab ochre colour of iron oxide. Everything was obviously welded together with rust. It didn't require an engineer of Stephens' calibre to work out that Ringing Rock was ready to join Morous on the shed floor.

Even the optimistic Managing Director looked crestfallen. He climbed into the cab, in the process dislodging a feathered resident that fluttered into the rafters squawking abuse.

"Hallet" he boomed.

"Yes sir," replied the miserable subordinate.

"Hallet – get Taffy to do me an omelette for lunch will you." He handed down two warm fresh eggs. At that moment there was a whistle from further up the line. It was the Hesperus pulling two ancient coaches separated by an open topped wagon. The wagon contained the train's only paying passenger, a red-faced farmer with a sheepdog and a dozen sheep. As the Colonel watched in astonishment the farmer lifted the dogs and sheep one by one on to the platform where they ran off to all points of the compass before the dog was dispatched to round them up. It took much 'Come-by-Glen' type whistling, some barking and hand-to-hoof battles on the station platform before the small flock was rounded up. After dislodging a final couple of stragglers from the 'Ladies' toilet, the group noisily departed, through the ticket hall and station concourse and onto the cobbled lane beyond, leaving behind a trail of steaming black droppings. The locomotive Hesperus meanwhile, gasping for breath like an exhausted marathon runner, enveloped the platform in a cloud of acrid black smoke. When it cleared, it transpired there was another passenger after all. The farmer's wife, the sole occupant of the two coaches. She waved imperiously at Colonel Stephens, pointing at the station clock, "Late as usual", she said, before following the bleating/barking menagerie through the ticket hall. As she passed the office she pulled a string of sausages from the basket she was carrying and handed them to the clerk who, after glancing furtively at the Colonel, quickly spirited them out of sight. "Hallet" boomed Colonel Holman Stephens.

✷✷✷

Meanwhile in the office of the King's Private Secretary, another little drama was unfolding.

"I'm buggered if I'm attending some fly-blown do in – where did you say?"

"Selsey your Majesty".

It seemed the King was in a foul temper. He had had no luck lately with the horses and earlier that day, just when it looked like his favourite 'Anmer' was about to break with Royal tradition by winning the Epsom Derby, some 'dreadful Pankhurst woman' had thrown herself under its feet bringing it down.

The Secretary, Sir Arthur Penhalligan, tried again,

"I am afraid all the arrangements have already been made. You will recall it was at your Majesty's suggestion you spend a day or two at the seaside following your visit to Goodwood."

"Yes but I meant somewhere civilised. Brighton perhaps, Bognor even, not some God-forsaken glorified fishing village in the back of beyond."

Sir Arthur sighed,

"I have been to this village – a pleasant enough location. The Marine Hotel is quite… adequate for your purposes and the Mayor of Chichester has reputedly spent a considerable sum on the civic reception."

The King glowered in his beard,

"Bugger the civic reception. Find some excuse – anything will do – Clemence tells me the only road in and out of the place is a farm track full of pot holes."

"Clemence is mistaken. The highway is perfectly adequate," replied the King's secretary", however by way of transport I am told there is a railway – of sorts – which connects the village to the main line at Chichester. A total journey time, I am informed, of barely thirty minutes – so there is no reason for His Majesty to step outside the royal coach until we arrive there."

The King grunted something that may have been an oath but was more likely the resigned acceptance of monarchs to the sad burdens of office. Sir Arthur pressed home his advantage, "It need only be for one night. Nobody expects you to stay more than a couple of days. Anyway you may even like it."

The withering look suggested otherwise.

***

A ride on the Tram was one of the joys of Sussex rural life, if you weren't in hurry that is. Where else would your journey be interrupted so that the driver could stop and deliver parcels to remote farmsteads? Where else would the guard stop the train at every highway intersection because a bylaw required the train to be preceded over the road by someone waving a red flag? Where else would half the stations on the line be privately owned by local farmers as compensation for non-payment of land rent?

It is at one of these 'stations' we find Colonel Stephens.

"All I am asking is you give the shelter a coat of paint," he pointed towards a half-derelict lean-to at one end of the platform, "You never know, the King might just stop here and pay a visit."

"'Er only toilets are on up at the farm", said Farmer Grimmock.

"I didn't mean that sort of visit. I meant the Royal Party might want to pay their respects – you know – stop and say hello – who can tell?"

"Why'd 'er stop here? There's nought for 'em here. I've no time for any on 'em anyway. If I had my way we'd be a democracy like the yanks".

"We are a democracy. I think you mean a 'republic'. Anyway I'm not asking you to swear undying allegiance to the monarchy, merely make the place look a little more presentable. I'm obviously prepared", the words stuck in his throat, "to pay for some flowers to brighten up the ..." he looked around at the rotting heap of wooden sleepers and roofless shelter that comprised the private halt, "station", he finished.

Grimmock never let oft-proclaimed socialist principles stand in the way of business,

"That's fine Colonel. You should've said earlier. My wife can do some beautiful tub displays. Sells loads on 'em up at the shop. How many will you be needing? I'm sure I can get you a decent discount for bulk purchase. Let's see, how about six shillings a tub, four for a pound. Brighten your stations a treat."

Colonel Stephen's was by now far too weary to argue,

"All right, I'll take a dozen at 3 guineas – and for that you also paint the shelter?"

"A deal Colonel, provided you provide the paint? After all, 'er station'd look silly if it were done in different colours to rest on line."

Similar battles were to be fought the length of the Tramway before the full support of the company's infrastructure was assured.

Over the following days, unusually by Tramway standards, there was round the clock activity. Hesperus was oiled, cleaned and given a much needed coat of blue paint, her former livery visible only as flecks of green amongst the heaps of rust on the workshop floor. Platforms were swept and station signs polished or repainted in the same blue paint, purchased as a job lot for restoring the Hesperus. At each end of the platforms Grimmock's tubs were displayed; sad huddles of pansies, squinting over the ragged rims of old bitumen drums. In a rare burst of generosity the Colonel even offered a prize to any member of staff who made the most original contribution to the spirit of the preparations. First prize went to Taffy Tapholme, whose wife had woven a tapestry depicting the Hesperus , union jacks flying, crossing the nearby marsh causeway, with a headboard over the buffers bearing the inscription 'The Royal Flier'. Colonel Stephens handed out the prize himself, a set of wooden false teeth in a special presentation case inscribed 'May they serve you well.'

The idea of a back-up engine unfortunately had to be abandoned after a locomotive, borrowed from a sister line of the Colonel's railway empire, blew up during delivery blocking the main South Coast Railway line, whose director demanded, and was refused, an extortionate amount of compensation for the inconvenience.

Luckily the Hesperus had never been in better condition and there was general optimism amongst the staff. Colonel Stephens, to his delight, was inundated with offers of patronage from local businessmen, particularly for platform advertising, which he used to offset his considerable (at least by Tramway standards) outlays. These included a tempting offer from Stubbs of Stubb's Coal Merchants fame who turned up unannounced at the Tramway office carrying a sack of experimental boiler fuel he had recently patented that he wanted the Colonel to use in the engine pulling the royal train. The Colonel crushed one of the black briquettes in his hand dubiously,

"You sure this stuff works?"

Stubbs, who only had one eye, turned so that his good eye pointed away as he replied,

"You have my absolute guarantee. I'm even prepared to waive any charge for supply of same"

The Colonel crumbled another briquette in his hand,

"What is it?", he enquired warily.

Instead of replying, Stubbs reached inside his dirty gaberdine coat and produced an even dirtier but reassuringly thick wad of banknotes, "Just coal Colonel – just coal.

Obviously under the circumstances I am prepared to Offer something in the way of compensation for the small inconvenience to your good self in initiating this trial.In this instance to the tune of fifty p…"

"One hundred."

"Quite right – one hundred pounds"

After all, Stephens thought, there was no need to use it. Just carry it on the engine during the trip.

This was only one of many similar transactions, both legal and illegal, conducted over the following days.

The Colonel was so flush with money in the end he even magnanimously purchased new uniforms for all the station staff. As to his own ex-army uniform, it was cleaned and pressed and his medals polished so that they shone like rails on some other railway.

In short all was ready for the big day.

✱✱✱

Goodwood had never been a lucky course for King George V and today was not the exception. He went through the card, disastrous selection following disastrous selection, providing confirmation if such was needed, that he was as good at selecting decent racehorses as his own stable was at producing them. His humiliation was complete when his own horse, 'Verity', owing to an unexpected sudden attack of wind, unseated its rider shortly before the start of the main race of the day and he had to force a polite smile while presenting the 'King George V Stakes' prize to his arch rival, the Duke of Norfolk.

He was thus in a vile temper when the Royal Train, travelling down from Goodwood, pulled into Chichester, where the

Mayor and Lady Mayoress were waiting for him on the platform. The band of the Royal Engineers struck up with 'I do like to be beside the seaside', very popular in its day, as the King stepped down. It had started to rain, deepening the King's gloom, as he was paraded before an interminable number of local dignitaries. His mood was blacker than the thunder clouds gathered overhead.

***

In the nearby Tramway station, Hesperus was waiting patiently by the rail junction for the Royal summons. The engine had behaved surprisingly well but Driver Blackett had serious concerns about Stubb's briquettes.

They were a funny colour for one thing – stripy black and grey, like a badger's brow, and when he had attempted to burn one it burst apart with a loud report followed by a cloud of black smoke whilst generating little in the way of heat. The reason for this, it can now be disclosed, is that the briquettes were made from coal dust from Stubbs' yard, mixed with sufficient chalk to 'give them' in the words of the entrepreneurial fuel technologist 'oomph' The cautious Blackett had, as instructed, avoided using any of this coal substitute but had placed the alternative fuel prominently on the top of the bunker to advertise its presence. However, as Blackett waited for his signal (the National Anthem played by the Royal Engineers), who should appear but Stubbs himself accompanied by a local photographer. Stubbs was wearing Fireman Barnes' uniform since he had been given permission by Colonel Stephens to act as surrogate fireman for the trip, as part of the same deal negotiated for the novel fuel substitution. He squinted up at the driver.

"Blackett," he nodded.

"Stubbs", acknowledged Blackett, making no move to stand aside and let him on board.

"How's she burning?". He waved a coal blackened hand in the direction of his briquettes.

"Ah," replied the driver non-commitally.

"Good stuff. Been using them myself on the allotment."

"Ah," said Blackett.

"Bung some in then."

"Pardon?" said Blackett.

"Shove some on 'er briquettes in the boiler."

The photographer was setting up his tripod to record the historic moment.

The driver looked vainly up and down the platform for support and finding none reluctantly opened the firebox door staring dubiously at the sputtering flames.

"Go on then," encouraged Stubbs.

"Ah," said Blackett, making no movement.

"Out the way man. I'll do it," Stubbs climbed up into the cab then turned to face the camera and took a shovel full of briquettes from the bunker.

"I shouldn't…"

***

King George's legs hurt. His back hurt. He was wet through. He had lost a considerable sum at Goodwood. He was standing on a windswept station platform, in pouring rain, shaking hands with gibbering provincials he felt sure he wouldn't like even after he got to know them, assuming he was ever likely to meet any of them again. His sole consolation was that he was, at last, approaching the end of the interminable line of officials placed before him, and could shortly dash for the comfort, warmth and solitude of the royal coach. At this precise moment, however, a young woman broke free of the police cordon. She ran towards the King, her long skirt trailing in the puddles, hotly pursued by Constables Morris and Bligh of the Sussex Constabulary. Before Morris could fell her with an excellent if over-dramatic rugby tackle she had despatched two rotten eggs at the monarch, with the words,

"Women's suffrage."

The King surveyed the stinking mess that was his great coat. He surveyed the woman, now being led away, still screaming 'Votes for women', surveyed the rain and the bloated miserable faces of the Mayor and Mayoress of Chichester and prayed for a miracle.

His prayers were answered.

As the band struck up 'God save the King', the Hesperus detonated. It was said, that parts of the boiler were alter discovered high up the bell tower of the cathedral half a mile away. Driver Blackett and Coal Merchant Stubbs were located shaken but otherwise unhurt beneath the Tramway platform where they sought refuge after the steam pressure gauge blew. If the photographer's camera had survived he would have had the scoop of his career, Unfortunately, what was left of the camera was later found along with what was left of the photographer on top of a nearby gasometer.

For the first time that day King George smiled. His smile became a beam, then he laughed out loud,

"Home Stanfordham."

"But Your Highness what about Selsey?"

"Sod Selsey," said the King striding purposefully away.

Tour Bus

We wave to the buses – the tour buses. The tourists wave back. Hen parties from Halifax. Stag parties from Stoke. Fat Americans sporting fat American cameras. The tour guides get them all to wave to us. Guided tours of the Falls and Shankhill Roads. Open top trips to the Troubles. We drink our Guinness in the shadow of the masked men murals and wave back. This is our contribution to the 'peace dividend'. There's a cheer from the boyos at the bar. On the box the Chuckle Brothers, Paisley and Adams, pose for the cameras at the opening of a new 'Harvey Nicks'. Everything is better now we are told. Gone the union flags and the tricolour flagstones. All that history and hate buried in a coat of paint. The Court House in the Crumlin Road is to be a museum. The tunnel that linked the Court House to Crumlin Road Jail will be a gallery dedicated to those comrades who died. People are bidding on ebay for pieces of the Peace Wall. It's no longer possible to tell at a glance which side of the divide you're on.

But we know.
We the poor, the ignorant, the unemployed.
We know.
We wave to the tour buses but we do not go away.
We remember.
We wait.
Nothing changes.
No surrender.

Bombardment

Jackie threw the winch handle over and the serried ranks of nets shuffled slowly over the stern to fall with hardly a splash into the water behind 'Spion Kop'. From somewhere beyond the dense sea 'fret' a church bell was chiming 'five', the sound fading into the hiss of the swell at the edge of the harbour mouth. Charlie, the boat's only other crew member, started the engine and the fifteen-foot seine netter chugged forwards trailing its line of bobbing red and yellow floats, like some metallic water spider spinning an inch-thick rope web.

The fishing this year had been good. Onset of War had resulted in rising food prices, particularly the codling, mackerel and whiting which were the Spion Kop's principal catch. Good for the fisherman, not so good for the residents of Hartlepool. The weather had also been kind. The North Sea coast, notorious for autumnal gales, had been unseasonably quiet, as if to compensate for the ongoing conflict in Europe. Other than the bonus of high fish prices, however, the war had yet to have an impact on the Sotherans. True Jackie's eldest boy, David, had volunteered for the army but, until recently, he had only been posted to a training camp at Catterick and was unlikely to be sent oversees before the war ended, since the newspapers were claiming the war would be over by Christmas. For the last few weeks, moreover, David had been assigned, locally, to the heavy gun battery called the 'Heugh' (pronounced Yuff) on the promenade, facing the harbour entrance. Until the raw recruits were called up to the front they often served their time as part of a small garrison protecting local shipyard and docks. David was already at work on the early morning shift at the gun battery.

Jackie's other eight children had also had unexpected spin-off benefits from the war. For the first time, the boys were afforded the luxury of separate beds and the croft cottage, where they lived, now boasted a new metal stove, lovingly boot-blacked by Jack's wife Mary.

"Charlie – give us a hand with these boxes will yer?"

Charlie, barely fourteen and a new addition to the crew, stuck his head out of the small cabin window.

"Worrisit Jack?"

"Gerrout here yer idle beggar. Who do yer think yerrar, Admiral Nelson?"

Charlie reluctantly left the ship's wheel.

"See that clawhammer, well start pulling them old fish boxes to bits and see if any of the wood's any good for mending the broken crates."

Reluctantly the boy started to prise the fish box remnants apart, stacking the good wood to his right and dumping any unsalvageable timber over the side. He had barely started when the rest of the nets and floats on deck hurtled past him towards the stern. The netting snagged on the gunwale dragging the boat to a stop as the whine of the engine became a howl. Jackie and Charlie simultaneously lost their footing, slithering down the sloping deck towards the rear of the boat which was now sinking into the sea.

"For Chrissake, the nets have hooked. "

Jackie rushed to the stern, already shipping water, and kicked out with as much force as possible at the tangle of rope. The rail of the boat splintered as the nets tore away and the Spion Kop bobbed out of the water like a cork. With a yell Charlie went over the side, his skipper thrown violently back through the open cabin door. Grabbing the ships wheel he swung the boat about as the smothering sea fog closed in.

***

On a nearby beach Nan Boagey was gathering driftwood. Despite being one of the town's oldest residents she was always first down, often working alone in the dark, building up a small store of reusable timber at the bottom of the stone steps at the fisherman's gate through the town wall. Her two boys, Joe and Rob, would be round to collect the wood later, to sell intact – if in good condition – or more likely to tie up in bundles for sale as kindling. On her back she carried a woven wicker fish basket and every now and then she bent down to retrieve a length of sodden timber from the tangle of seaweed at the water's edge.

The sea fog, or 'fret', was especially thick and she shivered and tightened her shawl around her shoulders. The world was a swirling grey room, filled with ghostly shadows.

She tried singing to herself in her thin croaky voice, "… and her name was Cushy Butterfield and she liked our beer.", the song punctuated by bells from the old Norman Church on the Headland tolling the hour.

She felt rather than heard the throb of a big ship's engines coming through the mist from the harbour mouth and she walked out to the towards the sea trying to identify the cause. Surely no-one was attempting to dock in this mist?

As she reached the edge of the tide she thought she saw an enormous dark shadow against the white curtain of fret. If it was a ship it was bigger than the usual timber and coal merchantmen that used the harbour. The wake of a ship rolled in at waist height carrying her up the beach and depositing against the stone of the town wall. It rolled away, leaving her a heap of wet rag on the draining sand.

✶✶✶

Mary Sotheran was preparing breakfast for Sammy and Laurie her teenage boys, both dock workers. A network of mines across the north filled the holds of the collier boats that fuelled the engines of the greatest Empire the world had ever seen. Rails were suspended out over the sea, lifted beyond the reach of the waves the waves on wooden piers or staithes, so that the coal could be delivered to the colliers without further handling. Mary's sons, about to leave for work, were part of a team of carpenters who swarmed like monkeys over the weed and shellfish encrusted timbers of the staithes, sometimes working just inches above the water in the dock. The work was hard and dangerous and the men's lives were short. Still, the money was good in an area where full employment only arrived with the onset of war.

Breakfast today consisted of bread and dripping or 'bread and dip' as local people called it. It was bread and dip yesterday and it would be bread and dip tomorrow. Occasionally the bread was fried but usually it was just dipped in animal fat which Mary obtained for next to nothing from the butchers. At weekends there might be a treat, sausages or even (recently) bacon and eggs but during the week it was always 'bread and dip'. The boys accepted this without complaint, only grumbling when Mam's money didn't run to 'dip'.

"What's for bait Mam?", Sammy asked, leaning over his mother's shoulder as she cut hunks off the loaf.

"I got some mops". Rolled 'mops' were smoked herrings soaked in oil. Being a fisherman's wife there was usually some sort of fish. It was meat that was scarce. The boy's sandwiches were carefully arranged in metal boxes with a faded picture of Queen Victoria and crossed union jack flags on the cover. These were their 'bait boxes' or 'snap tins' and the boys could vary the fare by trading one of their fish sandwiches with their mates (or marrers) for meat or egg.

The baby started crying – beginning with a few staccato coughs which became a hungry howl that woke the other children. The youngest slept in one bed, inset like an oven in the croft cottage wall. Sammy and Laurie, as 'workers', who contributed to the income of the house, had the luxury of their own beds, made up on the floor of the living room after the evening meal had been cleared. The only other room in the property was Jack and Mary's bedroom which was just large enough for a double bed, a dresser and a wooden chair.

After packing the girls Kitty and Patty off to school Mary sat down to nurse the baby while the other children dressed themselves. Kitty and Patty, who were eight and six respectively, went to the infant's school called the 'Prisick' on a steep hill overlooking the north facing beach on the Headland. The school was only open in the mornings. There was no school for Crofters older than twelve years. Teenagers went to work in the shipyards, if boys, or took fishing industry jobs such as gutting and cleaning fish on the harbour side, if girls. During the day the toddlers played outside with other children of the same age. There was no danger from traffic – not even a horse and cart could negotiate the narrow alleyways that separated the back-to-back houses that constituted the 'Croft'. Mary went to the door to look for David who usually arrived home around this time.

A burst of gunfire from the battery broke the silence. Practise firing, on those rare occasions it was scheduled, always took place in the middle part of the day. Mary hurried out into the street. Front doors were opening along the road. Housewives, with hair tied up in working turbans, were spilling out of their front doors, looking in the direction of the Heugh.

Why were the guns being fired?

***

It had been the usual quiet night in the gun battery. Whilst maintaining the pretence of being at war there was little, in truth, for the tiny garrison to do. Once the guns had been cleaned and oiled for the tenth time and the evening watch established, the rest of the men either slept or played cards. David Sotheran, fresh from training camp, was half of the night's acting 'watch'. Alongside him was his 'marrer', Private Theophilis (Taffy) Jones. Private Jones was a local man, like David, who had acquired the pseudonym 'Taffy' because of his surname rather than from any obvious Welsh ancestry.

"Can you see out, Taff?", David handed his mate a cup of tea.

"Bugger all". Private Jones clasped the cup gratefully in both hands to extract the maximum warmth from the drink, "What time is it?"

"About quarter to eight."

"Thank God for that. I thought the bloody night was goin' on forever."

"What yer doing later on?"

"Well after ah've restored me natural beauty with a few hours kip I dare say I shall peramborlate down the 'Cos' for a pint or nine." The 'Cosmopolitan' was the 'squaddies' pub. Strict demarcation lines existed for local clientele. The 'Harbour of Refuge', for example, was frequented mainly by dockers (and prostitutes) and the 'Globe' by tradespeople. Women, other than the 'ladies of the night', never used the pubs, preferring to buy cheap gin from the off-license. Jones, a ruddy faced youth looking more like a farm labourer than a regular soldier, had joined the army because of peer pressure rather than personal conviction. He was an only child and reputedly spoilt by his parents. He also had a reputation with the local girls of always having money to spend and was, unsurprisingly, popular.

"Are you coming down for a game of 'arrers' later on?"

David shook his head, "Ah've got nowt 'til I get paid on Friday – anyway I thought you was tashin' Beryl from Durham Street."

"She went off with Phil Bines didn't she."

"What, spotty Phil from the Co-op?"

"The same – there's no 'countin' for taste is there?"

"What the…"

The first shell from the 'Seydlitz' landed short, some hundred metres from the battery. The second was a direct hit on the six-inch gun emplacement where the two men were standing. Sotheran was bruised but otherwise unhurt, despite being hurled ten metres across the room. Jones was less fortunate. David found his friend seated upright in the centre of a pile of rubble that had been the gun placement. His expression was one of amazement, as he stared sightlessly out to sea through the new hole in the concrete wall of the battery. The back of his head was scattered amongst the debris on the floor. Private Theophilis Jones had acquired the dubious honour of being the first British soldier of the war to die on English soil.

✶ ✶ ✶

The men on the platforms beneath the coal staithes downed tools.

"What the hell's goin' on gaffer?" Laurie Sotheran shouted up to his foreman about four metres above his head.

"I'm buggered if I know Lol – sounds like there's firing at the Heugh."

"The' wouldn't be taking pot shots at anything in fret this thick would they – unless something was up."

"Is your Dave on duty?" Billy McAvoy, the lead carpenter, had noticed the concern in the boy's voice.

Before Laurie could answer a shell struck the staithes halfway between the men and the land, removing a fifteen-metre section of timber, yet leaving the rails intact like a wire bridge between the remaining halves of the structure. Two loaded coal wagons still hung in the air, suspended on the unsupported rails. The intended target, however, had not been the coal staithes for no more shells landed nearby. Instead they whistled and howled overhead.

"The buggers are aiming for the shipyard – Gerrup here – Lol, Tom."

The young men scrambled up the rungs, installed like huge metal staples at three-foot intervals in the thick wooden props. Above them McAvoy was already on the railway. Pausing to help the boys up he set off on a loping run towards the shore, carefully matching his stride to the sleeper separation between the rails. Behind him the boys, struggled to keep up, tripping and stumbling as they ran. When McAvoy reached the missing section of the staithes he stepped confidently on to the suspended rail and walked confidently out over the gap. The others took the more sensible course of shuffling across on their backsides. The rail sagged alarmingly under the combined weight of the three men and they had barely reached the other side when one of the supporting timbers behind them splintered and fell slowly away, crashing into the black waters of the dock. Something was worrying McAvoy about the nature of the gunfire. The shells screaming over their heads weren't matched by the sounds of impact in the dockyard.

"By God the bastards are firin' on the town as well."

"They cannot be. What for? There's nowt to shoot at 'cept people's houses. Christ – me Mam's there"

Laurie overtook his boss and reaching the end of the staithes first, jumping down on to the shingle beach. Within seconds he had reached the wooden jetty on the harbour side, where a rowboat was moored. Overhead the first rays of sun were penetrating the gloom. To get from the docks to the Headland meant crossing the narrow harbour entrance. Laurie jumped into the boat, grabbed the oars and began to row furiously towards the Fisherman's Gate. The sound of guns increased with every stroke until they became deafening. He turned instinctively towards the source of the noise. Looming through the mist, and completely blocking the harbour entrance was a German battle cruiser, the 'Blucher', her eight portside guns firing steadily and randomly into the narrow streets of the Croft.

At the Prisick Infants School, on hearing the first sound of gunfire, the elderly Headmistress, Mrs. Rackstraw, ordered all the children outside where a rapid roll call revealed that two children were unaccounted for. One of the teachers was despatched to look for them whilst the headmistress led the others away from the built-up part of the town towards the comparative safety of the beach. The sky now shimmered in the flickering light of a hundred fires, periodically brightening as another shell exploded.

"Form lines. Hold hands with the person next to you. Don't run. Don't cross the road 'til I say so."

The zip and bang of bursting shells got louder as the cruiser extended its range; the target now being the gas works on the far side of the docks. Mrs. Rackstraw watched in horror as flames began to lick up the side of the gasometer.

"Get down children!"

The shock wave threw her off her feet as the huge tank literally disappeared. In an instant the buildings to either side also vanished in clouds of smoke and flame. Some of the children began crying – others clung on tightly to their friends.

"Quiet please – *I said quiet*."

The children's cries reduced to sobs and sniffles.

Mrs. Rackstraw, blood streaking her grey hair, rose to her feet.

"Follow me. Hold hands with the person next to you. Quickly now. Don't run. Move." Shells were falling around and behind her and the Prisick was burning.

✷✷✷

The school consisted of just three rooms: a reception area where textbooks were kept: a small staffroom shared by two teachers and the headmistress and the 'class' were all lessons were conducted. The classroom, which faced the sea, had taken a direct hit. Patty Sotheran had been taking her younger sister to use the outside toilet and returned to find the school deserted. She went to look for the other children and had just entered the main entrance to the school when she was bowled over by the force of the explosion which demolished the classroom behind her. Picking herself up she grabbed her screaming sister by the scruff of her neck and crawled under a table. Mrs. Horsburgh, Patty's teacher, who had entered the classroom from a side door was killed instantly. Within seconds the whole of the timber framed building was aflame.

A mile away Vice Admiral Hipper, of the Seydlitz, focussed his binoculars on the shore battery. The armour piercing shells had undoubtedly inflicted major damage on the Heugh but the defending garrison, far from being neutralised were redoubling their efforts and the Blucher, being the nearest target, had sustained some superficial damage. Hipper had planned to keep the third of his cruisers, the Moltke, in reserve in case they had to engage enemy ships but he now decided that all efforts must concentrate on neutralising the battery if the Blucher was to extricate herself safely from the harbour.

Hipper had disliked the assignment from the outset. A man of honour, the idea of a civilian strike as a propaganda exercise, was repugnant to him. Waging war against soldiers was one thing, killing defenceless women and children, in his opinion, was both pointless and self-defeating. Nothing, he believed, enervated an opposing army more than an attack deliberately targeted against innocent people. Nonetheless, grim though the operation was, he saw it as his duty to carry it out with the minimum loss of life to the crew of the ships under his command.

"Call up the Moltke. I want those guns on the headland silenced before the Blucher disengages."

He raised his binoculars again towards the concrete blockhouse on the shore.

Less than three hundred metres away, on the far side of a rocky beach, his opposite number, Lieutenant Colonel Robson of the Durham Royal Garrison Artillery had a difficult decision to make. Only two of the battery's five guns had survived the attack and much of the stations meagre supply of ammunition had either been lost or used. Additionally, of the fourteen men stationed at the Heugh four were dead and four others seriously injured. He knew he needed to concentrate his remaining fire on the Blucher, whose guns were inflicting so much damage on the defenceless town, but by re-directing his limited weaponry away from the Seydlitz he would leave the battery itself defenceless Also, he wasn't sure of the range of the guns on the battle cruisers. There was, he felt, the distinct possibility that the bombardment would continue from the open sea anyway. To add to everything else the Blucher was an awkward target as it faced the battery face on. Any further thoughts on the matter were interrupted by the crash of dozens of shells falling around the station as the Moltke joined the fight.

On the bridge of the Seydlitz Hipper noted, with satisfaction, that the barrage from the shore battery had finally ceased.

✯✯✯

Hot acrid black smoke filled the room, dense near the ceiling where paint bubbled up and fell in fiery droplets on to the table under which the children were hiding.

"My eyes hurt. Can we go now our Pat?"

Kitty Barnes shook her older sister awake.

Patty sat up banging her head and unable to reply until she had coughed all the soot from her lungs.

"We have to stay here Kitty until Mrs. Horsburgh says it's safe."

"But I want to go home now."

"No – they'll be here any minute – you watch if they don't."

Patty rocked backwards and forwards holding her quietly sobbing sister tightly in her arms like her favourite doll,

"There – there."

A tongue of flame flashed across the ceiling.

"There – there."

"Patty – *Patty* – is that you?"

"Lol – it's Lol"

"Patty – where are you?"

"Here – in here – with our Kitty."

"Hang on."

✶ ✶ ✶

As soon as he went through the sea gate in the town wall Laurie immediately encountered his mother pushing the two infants in a battered pram loaded with possessions collected at random before she left the house. The streets were crowded with townspeople stripping their homes of anything valuable and putting their belongings on to handcarts. A crocodile of women and children were already heading out of the town along the single road that led off the headland to the safety of the countryside.

"Are you awright Mam?"

"Lol – I heard they hit the gas works. That's right next to the Prisick. Can you go see the girls are safe?"

Laurie fought his way through the tide of refugees leaving the town. It was less than two hundred metres to the school but it took him a good 20 minutes before he finally arrived. The area was barely recognisable. A circular open space the size of a football field surrounded the jagged remnants of the gasometer, where pockets of gas still flared intermittently from burst pipes. Half the Prisick had gone, with the roof of the solitary classroom ablaze.

"Laurie." It was Mrs. Snowdon, one of the teachers from the school," all the children are down on the beach safe except Patty and Kitty. Maude was sent back to look for them but she hasn't returned."

Laurie crossed quickly over the playround to the main entrance to the school. Although the only part of the school relatively undamaged he found he was unable to open the door leading into the classroom which had warped in the heat. He threw all his weight against it to force it open and burst into the room as the air above his head ignited. As he hit the ground he heard the children screaming. Crawling through smoke he located an arm.

"Thank Christ." He dragged Pat, still holding on to her sister backwards and out of the door as a tongue of flame fell to the floor.

✶✶✶

Admiral Scheer of the Blucher had been informed about the tiny fishing boat to starboard but had dismissed it as being of no consequence. The Blucher was at anchor, armour plated and impervious to any external danger other than that from another battleship. Hence he was totally unprepared when the Blucher began to rotate around its anchor.

***

Jackie Smith knew his boat couldn't hurt the Blucher but that had never been his intention. He nudged the Spion Kop up against the stern of the cruiser and revved the engines for all they were worth. The battleship, despite its enormous bulk slowly began to turn, held fast by the anchor chain. Before the German commander could react the great fighting ship became wedged across the deep water channel at the harbour entrance – square on to the guns of the Heugh. The timing could not have been better. Shells from the battery immediately tore into the Blucher cutting a hole the size of a house in her port side and destroying the stern guns. At that instant the sky lit up as flares were fired from the Seydlitz. The Blucher had been ordered to withdraw. With a series of grinding crunches the fighting ship weighed anchor and turned into the deep water channel and made out to sea as fast the engines would permit.

The bombardment was over It had lasted less than fifty minutes.

***

On 16th December 1914 three German battleships entered the port of Hartlepool and bombarded the old town and shipyard. The action which lasted less than an hour resulted in the deaths of 121 people and injured more than 400. Amongst the dead was Private Theophilis Jones the first fatality of the Great War to die on British soil. The small garrison commanding the shore battery, despite being heavily outgunned, kept up a continuous fire and were commended for exceptional gallantry. Lieutenant Colonel Robson, commanding, was awarded the DSO.

END

Printed in Poland
by Amazon Fulfillment
Poland Sp. z o.o., Wrocław